"Where is he?" Christopher's low voice resonated in her ears.

"Get out of here," Jasmine said, hurt and anger warring within her.

"Not until I've seen my son."

"*Your* son? *Your* son is doing very well without you. When did you decide to be a daddy, Christopher? Yesterday?"

Some things hadn't changed, Christopher thought. Jasmine Enderlin was as pigheaded as she'd always been. If she hadn't jumped to conclusions a year ago, he wouldn't be standing here like a stranger on her front porch. If God had been willing, they would have been married.

But God wasn't willing. And Jasmine wasn't budging.

He'd been so certain he was meant to come back. He loved Jasmine. He always had. And though he knew he had a long way to travel to get back in her good graces, it had to be done. He needed Sammy in his life.

Sammy—and Jasmine.

Books by Deb Kastner

Love Inspired

A Holiday Prayer #46
Daddy's Home #55

DEB KASTNER

The wife of a Reformed Episcopal minister, Deb naturally found her niche in the Christian/inspirational romance market. She enjoys tackling the issues of faith and trust within the context of a romance. Her characters range from upbeat and humorous to (her favorite) dark and brooding heroes. Her plots fall anywhere between, from a playful romp to the deeply emotional.

When she's not writing, she enjoys spending time with her husband and three girls and, whenever she can manage, attending regional dinner theater and touring Broadway musicals.

Daddy's Home
Deb Kastner

Love Inspired®

Published by Steeple Hill Books

STEEPLE HILL BOOKS

Steeple
Hill™

ISBN 0-373-87055-8

DADDY'S HOME

Copyright © 1999 by Debra Kastner

Printed in U.S.A.

He has showed you, O man, what is good.
And what does the Lord require of you?
To act justly and to love mercy and to walk humbly
with your God.

—Micah 6:8

To my daddy, Jim Larkin,
for never letting me give anything but my best.
And for my girls' daddy, Joseph C. Kastner, Jr.,
who never stopped believing.

Chapter One

"Christopher's back in town."

Jasmine Enderlin stiffened at the statement. Keeping a carefully neutral expression on her face, she met her grandmother's shrewd gaze. "And you're telling me this because...?"

"Don't be obtuse," Gram snapped, shaking a wrinkled finger under Jasmine's nose. "Don't you pretend I need to spell it out for you. I'm not buying. You know exactly what I'm saying, and you know why. Now, do you want to know the details, or don't you?"

"Yes," she whispered, not even sure Gram would hear her. She released an audible sigh and turned back to the thick olive-colored sweater she'd been folding moments before.

Jenny's sweater.

Brushing the soft material across her cheek, she caught a whiff of Jenny's light, breezy scent on it.

She wouldn't have thought something as simple as the smell of her sister's perfume would set her off, but for some reason, today it did. Her eyes pricked with tears, and she brushed them away with a hurried swipe of her fist, hoping Gram wouldn't notice the furtive action.

Why would Christopher come back to Westcliffe at all, and especially now of all times?

As if to answer Jasmine's unspoken question, Gram shrugged her age-bent shoulders. "He wants his son."

"What?" She sprang from the bed, tipping a pile of freshly folded blue jeans into a heap at her feet. "What do you mean he *wants* Sammy? He can't have him," she added vehemently, hugging her arms to her chest as if protecting an infant there. *Her* infant.

A moment more and she would have dashed from the room to snatch up the baby boy sleeping soundly in his bassinet in the next bedroom, but Gram held up a finger in protest. "You haven't heard the story."

I know the story, she thought, her heart clenching. *Love. Betrayal. Desertion.*

That chapter of her life was over, she reminded herself, fiercely determined to remain in control of her emotions. She shook her head to detour the advancing thought, but it came anyway.

Jenny's dead.

Ugliness folded over her like quicksand. God didn't help Jenny. He could have, but He didn't. Guilt stabbed at her conscience, and she briefly wondered if her thoughts constituted blasphemy.

Maybe they did.

But how could she change the way she felt, the way she viewed things? What else was she to think? Three months ago when *she* hadn't been able to save Jenny. Not with all her years of medical training, not with so much love that she would have willingly taken her sister's place.

And God had done nothing.

"It isn't your fault, my dear," Gram said as she hobbled over to a high-backed Victorian chair and seated herself with the sluggishness of age. "You shouldn't blame yourself."

Gram, she reflected with an inward wince, had the annoying ability to read her mind. Even as a child when Jasmine lost both parents to a tragic car accident, Gram had known what she was thinking and feeling. Gram had raised her, knew better than anyone what she suffered now.

"Because Christopher came back all of a sudden, after a year away?" she asked, knowing full well it was not the question Gram was answering.

Her keen silver eyes fixed upon Jasmine. If she was disturbed by her granddaughter's persistent avoidance of the obvious, it didn't show in her gaze.

"I had my hair set in the salon today," she said,

relating the story as if it were of no consequence. As if Jasmine's world hadn't come crashing to a halt the moment she'd heard Christopher's name. "Lucille Walters came in for a perm. She told me everything she knew. Said since it's January and all, he's looking for a new beginning. Clean slate, you might say. Seems he's bunking with her boys at the Lazy H."

"He's rooming with ranch hands?" she asked, surprise sounding in her voice. His parents, like hers, were with the Lord. And as an only child, he had no family to return to. But ranch hands?

"Seems a bit peculiar to me." Gram raised a gray eyebrow and cocked her head to one side.

Her laughter was dry and bitter. "Yeah, for someone who's scared to death of horses, I'd say it is." How quickly the old anger returned to course through her. Righteous indignation swelled in her chest. She embraced it, welcoming the heat that surged through her bloodstream like electricity.

It was her way of dealing with what she couldn't stand to face. Anger filled the empty spaces, leaving no room for more painful, tender emotions to surface.

It was a welcome relief. "Did you talk to him?" she queried, her voice unusually low and scratchy.

"No." Gram leaned forward and cupped a hand to her mouth as if to whisper a secret. "But he told Lucille he wants his son."

"Sammy is *not* his son!"

Sammy! Would Christopher take him away from her? That sweet baby had given new meaning to her life, given her a reason to live when all she wanted to do after Jenny's death was crawl into the nearest hole and die.

And Christopher could take it all away. The thought pierced her heart like a stake. Sure, she had the papers that said she was Sammy's legal guardian, but Christopher was related by blood. She pumped her fists open and closed to release the tension swirling through her.

Oh Jenny. Why did God take you away from us?

"Sammy's *my* son," she said again, more to reassure herself than to answer Gram.

"Not sure the law will see it your way." Gram's age-roughened voice broke into her thoughts. Her eyes were full of compassion as she reached forward to squeeze her granddaughter's hand. "Seems to me Christopher had some part in making that baby."

Jasmine didn't want to think about that. "Jenny's will makes *me* his guardian. Besides, a romp in the sack doesn't make a man a father." She snorted her derision. "He doesn't deserve to be a father to baby Sammy, as I'm sure the courts will agree. He abandoned Jenny long before his *son* was born. What kind of a *father* does that make him?"

Gram held up her hands as if to ward off a blow. "I'm not disagreeing with you, honey. No-sirree! I'm just concerned that he's going to fight you every step of the way. Mark my words! You know as well as I do that Christopher Jordan is a strong, stubborn man. He won't stop until he gets what he wants.''

She knew. Better even than Gram did. Once, she'd known his heart and soul. Or at least she thought she had. "He won't get Sammy," she vowed, her voice tight.

Gram raised an eyebrow. "Well, girl, I've gotta say you can be just as determined as any ol' man when you put your mind to it.'' She chuckled. "My money's on you.''

"Thank you for your confidence," she replied with a wry smile. "I'll fight him if I have to.'' No one would take Sammy away from her. *No one.* He was her baby now. And he was all she had left of Jenny.

Sammy's cry pierced the gray haze of rage and frustration that flooded Jasmine's mind. She dashed into the other bedroom and tucked the crying baby to her chest, speaking to him in an incoherent, soothing whisper.

At three months old, Sammy was already well able to make his desires known, she reflected with a smile. Not all the anger in the world could dim the gentle glow of love that filled her heart every time she held this sweet, precious child.

With the palm of her hand, she smoothed the tuft of light brown hair covering his head. He had a cowlick on the left side of his forehead. Just like his father.

Christopher.

She shook the thought away. "Gram, if I change Sammy's diaper, will you take him for a while? I want to go through the rest of Jenny's clothes before I quit for the night."

Gram came around the corner, smiling and cooing as she approached Sammy. "Let's get you changed, little fellow, so I can take you. Your Mommy needs to get some work done."

Mommy. Jasmine felt less awkward after three months, but still the term hovered in the corner of her consciousness, taunting her to prove herself. She wrapped a fresh diaper around Sammy's waist and pinned it securely, barely giving a thought to her actions.

Some things, at least, were beginning to come easier for her.

It was she who rose each night for the two o'clock feeding, she who burped and cuddled and changed the boy.

She hadn't planned to be anyone's mother. Not for years yet, in any case. If only...

"Don't you think you've done enough for one day?" Gram asked, reaching for the infant and bouncing him against her shoulder, patting his back in an age-old, soothing rhythmic gesture. "You have to go to work early tomorrow. Besides, you've been called out three evenings in a row. Can't the people around here stay out of trouble for a single night?"

She chuckled. "I don't mind, Gram. Really. That's why I went to medical school. I survived my residency with far less sleep than I get here. This town rolls up the carpet at six o'clock in the evening! In Denver, our worst hours were late at night."

"Bc that as it may," Gram argued, "things have changed. You've got a little one dependent on you. You need to keep yourself healthy. For Sammy's sake, Jasmine, if not your own."

She laughed. "Gram, I've never been sick a day in my life, and you know it. I rarely even catch a cold!"

"For Sammy's sake," the old woman repeated, kissing the infant's forehead.

Jasmine sighed. "For Sammy's sake. Everything I'm doing is for Sammy's sake. Not that I regret a minute of it." She stroked one finger down his feathery cheek, enjoying the loud giggle that erupted from him. Staring down at him now, her heart welled with love.

"Take care of my baby."

Her sister's voice echoed through her head as if it were yesterday, and not three months past. Would that fluttery, empty feeling in the center of her chest ever really go away, or would she eventually learn to live with it? It caught her unawares at the oddest moments.

She closed her eyes and took a deep breath to steady her quivering nerves. "I've got to get back to these sweaters, or I'll never get this done."

Gram settled herself on the rocking chair in the corner of the baby's room and adjusted Sammy on her lap. "We'll be fine, dear. Just don't be too long. I think he's hungry."

"I'm not surprised. That baby eats more than most kids twice his size," she commented as she moved into the opposite bedroom. "There's a bottle ready in the fridge if he gets too restless."

She eyed the open closet defensively. Jenny's clothes—blouses crammed haphazardly onto hangers, blue jeans rolled and stuffed on the shelf top above, the one dress she owned to wear for special occasions—beckoned to her.

She'd already put off this unpleasant task too long. The time had come for her to finish packing Jenny's things away and to sell the bungalow.

She reached up to the shelf above her head and tugged on a pile of jeans, which came fluttering down on top of her. Something solid hit her head, making a loud, clapping noise and stinging her skin where it slapped. She instinctively threw her arms over her to protect herself from being beaned with further projectiles, but none were forthcoming. It was just one book.

A book had been rolled up in a pair of jeans? That was something she didn't see every day. Curious, she reached to retrieve the errant missile.

A Bible. Jenny had a Bible, hidden away like a treasured possession. Somehow she'd assumed Jenny had left the faith, if her actions were anything to go by.

Curious, Jasmine thumbed the pages, recognizing

the flowing loops and curves in the margins as Jenny's handwriting. Even though Jenny said she hadn't made peace with God until the end of her life, this Bible obviously had held some significance for her. Bits of paper were carefully folded into the book, as well as a single white rose, carefully pressed and dried, softly folded onto the page with the family tree.

Jasmine brushed her fingers over the crisp, dry calligraphy. "February twenty-fifth. Jennifer Lynn Enderlin married Christopher Scott Jordan."

Tears burned in her throat, and she bit her lip to keep them from flowing. Would the pain never lessen?

She ran a finger over the black ink, the carefully formed letters. Jenny's handwriting had always been so much neater than her own. It had been a source of endless amusement for Jenny to be able to harass her older sister about the chicken-scratching she passed off as handwriting. It was, she had often teased, God's sure sign to her that Jasmine was meant to be a doctor.

She curled up on the floor against the edge of the bed, staring at the Bible. It was a tangible piece of Jenny. She could run her fingers down the cracked leather binding, read the notes Jenny made in the margins about the Scriptures she read.

Slowly, almost reverently, she opened the Bible, silently flipping page after page, pausing to read a comment here and a highlighted Scripture there.

Jenny had obviously spent a lot of time in the Word before her death. Jasmine's throat constricted around her breath.

The doorbell sounded. She snapped the book shut and stuffed it under Jenny's pillow. Her thoughts whirlwinded as she considered who might be at the door. Perhaps someone was here to look at the bungalow, even though it wasn't listed yet.

"I'll get it!" she whispered, peeking into the extra bedroom. Sammy was sound asleep in Gram's arms, and it appeared Gram, too, had taken the liberty of a small nap. Her chin nestled against the baby boy, and her mouth had dropped open with the light buzz of snoring.

Jasmine chuckled quietly and moved to the front door. It was only when her hand was already on the knob and she'd half opened the door that it occurred to her who might be waiting.

"Christopher!" Jasmine confirmed, staring up at the tall, ruggedly handsome man before her. "What are you doing here?"

Her heart skipped a beat, then thumped an erratic tempo in her throat, blocking her breath. Anger, shock and a dozen other emotions buzzed through her like a swarm of angry bees.

A smile tugged at the corner of his mouth, but it didn't reach his eyes, which gleamed like cold, gray stones. Despite herself, Jasmine remembered how those eyes used to twinkle, changing in shade from a deep gray to a cobalt blue whenever he was happy.

He clearly wasn't happy now. The quirk of a smile changed into a frown, matching the twin creases between his light brown eyebrows.

"That's a fine welcome for an old...friend," he commented slowly, his scowl darkening.

"What do you want?" she snapped, her voice cold. She felt a stab of guilt for her rudeness, but she brushed it away.

The man didn't deserve better. In her book, anyone who deserted his family didn't deserve much of anything. Except maybe a swift kick in the backside.

"Cut to the chase, Christopher." The determined gleam in his eyes left no doubt he wasn't here for a social call. And the sooner he was gone, the better.

Every muscle in her body had tensed to the point of physical pain, but that was nothing in comparison to the wrenching agony of her heart at seeing him again. She had no idea it would be this difficult to face the man she'd once loved with all her heart. She clenched her fists, her fingernails biting into her palms.

I'm not ready.

She knew she'd eventually have to confront him, but she'd hoped to be doing it on her terms, in her time, on her own turf. Three strikes and she was out before she even got a chance to bat.

He was taller than she remembered, with a lithe frame and broad shoulders. He curled a steel gray cowboy hat in his fists, leaving exposed the cowlick that made his light brown hair cock up just over his left eyebrow. She remembered once telling him it gave him a roguish appearance. He'd just laughed and shaken his head. Maybe if he'd known just how much she'd wanted to spend her life with him—to marry him and raise a family with him—things might have been different. If only...

"Medical school has done wonders for your manners," he commented gruffly. "What do they teach you there? How to offend your neighbors in one easy lesson?"

The barbs found their mark. "You're not my neighbor." She scratched out the words, since her throat had suddenly gone dry.

He raised one eyebrow. "No? Whatever happened to the Good Samaritan? Or didn't you learn that one in church?"

Jasmine cringed inwardly. It wasn't like him to throw Scripture at her that way. He possessed a strong, quiet faith, which he neither took lightly nor tossed in someone's face like pearls before swine.

She wondered where that faith had gone. The past few months were proof of his decline. Choosing to marry Jenny over her without even the courtesy of a phone call, then up and abandoning the poor girl once she was carrying his child—the change was too great to fathom. The icy-eyed man standing before her was a virtual stranger.

"Maybe you haven't heard," he continued. "I'm living at Lucille's place now." He rolled the brim of his hat once more, then jammed it on his head.

"With the ranch hands," she added dryly.

"Mmm. So you did know, then. I was wondering how long it would take for the news to get back to you. Small town and all." He peered over her shoulder into the room. "Aren't you going to invite mc in?"

She heard Sammy cry out, and wondered if Christopher heard it, as well. With lightening swiftness, she stepped out onto the front porch and quietly but firmly closed the door behind her.

"No. I'd rather not." She wondered if he heard the quavering in her voice, and determined to control it with all the force of her will.

Christopher appeared unaffected by her intentional rudeness. He placed a hand on the door frame above her right shoulder and leaned into her, his face only inches from her own.

Her head spinning, she tried to inhale, tried to steady herself mentally. Instead, she breathed a heady whiff of his western-scented cologne.

Her favorite. The brand he used to wear especially for her.

Panicking, she stepped backward until her shoulders hit the solid strength of the door. This furtive movement was no deterrent for Christopher, who simply crooked his elbow to narrow the distance between them.

The brim of his hat touched her forehead, and he tilted his head to move in closer. His breath mingled with hers, his steel gaze never leaving hers for a moment.

She felt the way a mouse must feel when hypnotized by a snake's haunting eyes—knowing she would be consumed, yet powerless to look away.

He was going to kiss her. The snake wasn't even going to ask. Just take. And she wouldn't be able to stop him, so mesmerized was she by his gleaming eyes that looked so serious beneath the brim of his hat.

She closed her eyes. Despite her head screaming to the contrary, her heart beckoned him closer. It wasn't rational; in fact, it was quite out of the question. But knowing that didn't stop her from wanting his lips on hers just one last time. Perhaps it was a move toward resolution. She leaned closer, anticipating the moment their lips would meet.

"Where is he?" His low voice resonated in her ears.

Her eyes snapped open to meet his amused gaze. The twinkle had returned, and the dimple in his left cheek was showing. He was completely relaxed, and he was smirking at her!

Hurt and anger warring within her, she pushed both hands into his chest and shoved as hard as she could.

Christopher stepped back, but only because he wanted to. He didn't want to admit that his feelings hadn't changed, not in all these years, and not with all that had happened between them.

But now was not the time to pursue his feelings, though surely that time would arrive. He would *make* that time come, one way or another.

There were bridges to be built to gap the distance between them, and that would take some time. He'd known from the moment he decided to return to Westcliffe that it wouldn't be easy. Not for him, and most definitely not for Jasmine.

She could be one stubborn woman, he thought, pressing his lips together. But then again, he was a stubborn man. He clamped his teeth down hard and stared her down.

"Get out of here, you snake." Her voice was a low rasp.

Snake? He cringed inwardly at her animosity. He'd hoped her anger at the situation would have dulled enough with time for her to listen to reason, but it was obvious she was no closer to being ready to accept the truth than she'd been a year ago. He set his jaw and narrowed his eyes on her. "Not until I've seen my son."

"*Your* son? *Your* son is doing very well without you, thank you very much. When did you decide to be a daddy, Christopher? Yesterday? It's not like a hat that you can put on whenever you please. What right do you have to waltz in and demand to see him? He's a twenty-four-hour-a-day responsibility, which I have been facing alone, I might add. He's a flesh-and-blood human being, not some toy you can play with whenever the urge strikes you!"

"Yeah," he agreed, tipping his hat backward and raking his fingers through his hair. Some things hadn't changed.

Jasmine Enderlin was as pigheaded as she'd always been. If she hadn't jumped to conclusions a year ago, he wouldn't be standing here like a stranger on her front porch. God willing, they would've been married.

But God wasn't willing. And Jasmine wasn't budging.

"Give me a break, Jazz. I've been busting my tail to get back here."

"Is that so?" she snapped. bracing her arms on her hips. "And I'm supposed to feel sorry for you because you worked so hard to get back here?"

He leveled his gaze on her and stepped forward. "That's *so*," he said, his tone hard. "And at the moment, I don't give a wooden nickel how you feel about me. I want to see my son. Now."

Chapter Two

Jasmine's breath came in short, uneasy gasps. Her head swirled with emotion. To have to see Christopher again, to face not only what he'd done to her heart, but to her family, was enough to daunt the strongest of women. But to have him waltz into town and demand to see his child with all the arrogance of the perfect father was positively the last straw.

Anger welled in her chest.

"What right do you have to demand *anything?*" she growled through clenched teeth, willing her throbbing heart to slow before it beat a hole through her chest.

Christopher pulled the hat down low over his brows and leaned toward her, his posture firm and menacing. For a minute he just stared at her, the ice in his gaze freezing her insides. When he finally spoke, it was in a whisper. "I'm his father, Jazz."

His voice cracked on her name, and for the briefest moment, she saw a flicker of pain cross his gaze, so deep and intense she almost felt sorry for him.

Without even realizing what she was doing, she reached out a hand to stroke his strong jaw, then withdrew it just as quickly, curling her fingers into her chest as if she'd been burned.

She didn't feel *anything* for Christopher Jordan, she reminded herself harshly. Not anymore. He didn't deserve her pity, or her compassion. Scriptural verses flooded her mind, words about mercy and forgiveness, but she refused to concede. Not for him.

It didn't take a genius to read the change in her demeanor, and his eyes quickly shaded, resuming the tint of frosty steel.

"I have rights," he reminded her, his voice as cold as his gaze.

Jasmine steeled her heart, preparing to do mental battle with the man who'd once been the love of her life. She'd fight him tooth and nail for Sammy, and in the end, that was all that mattered. Not the past. The good or the bad. She wouldn't let her heart betray her a second time.

"You lost any rights you had the night you left Jenny alone and pregnant," she snarled.

His lips thinned. He opened his mouth to speak, then abruptly shut it again.

"You *aren't* Sammy's father," she added abruptly, sensing her advantage.

The barb met its mark, if his sharp intake of breath was any indication. She rushed on before she lost her nerve.

"You can threaten me with a lawsuit if you want, but I'm not backing down. Jenny made *me* Sammy's guardian. I've got papers to prove it—papers that will stand up in *any* court of law."

Jasmine wasn't as certain of her claim as she sounded, but she wasn't about to let on. She made a mental note to speak with the family attorney, feeling pleased that she'd struck Christopher dumb, at least for a moment.

He swept off his hat, his gaze genuinely hurt and confused. "Who said anything about a lawsuit?" he demanded, blowing out a breath. "Shoot, Jazz, don't you know me well enough by now to know I wouldn't do that to you? Or to Sammy," he added, under his breath.

Hat in hand, he reached out his arms to her, beseeching her with his gaze as well as his posture. "Just let me see him. I won't stay long. I just want to see that he's safe and—" His voice choked, cutting his sentence short. "Please, Jasmine. Just for a minute."

She felt herself relenting even as her answer left her lips. "Forget it. Not now, and not ever. Go back from whatever rock you crawled out from under, Christopher. There's nothing here for you now."

Her heart felt like it had been through a paper shredder, and she whirled away from him before she gave in to the earnest pleading in his tone. She had to get away from him until she could think things through, knowing she couldn't put two straight thoughts together when he looked at her that way.

How could she not remember the man Christopher once was, the strong, gentle man she loved? But that man was gone, her dreams shattered by the same disheartening reality that was responsible for creating the sweet little boy in the bedroom.

Which only served to prove that good really could come from something bad.

No matter what, she had to protect Sammy. She opened the screen door and slipped inside, glancing behind her shoulder in time to see Christopher punch his hat on his head and move to follow her.

Her heart pounded as she reached for the door and slammed it behind her, barely locking Christopher out before he began pounding.

"And good riddance," she whispered, leaning her forehead on the door.

Jasmine was terrified Sammy would wake up and start wailing. If that happened, and Christopher heard his baby, he'd never leave. She slid down against the wall, cupping her hands over her ears. Why wouldn't he just go away and leave them alone?

After ten minutes, when she'd finally concluded he'd never quit pounding, she heard him stomp back to his truck and slam the door. She felt both relieved and yet strangely desolate now that she was once again alone.

Her heart was still in her throat as she peeked from behind the front curtain and watched him drive away in his old Chevy truck, relaxing only when she knew for sure he was gone.

He would be back. Christopher Jordan was a stubborn, vigorous man who actively pursued what he wanted. He wouldn't let this episode stop him from seeing Sammy. But at least it would give her time to think, to sort out her feelings so she could face him again without the emotions that earlier clouded her judgement.

Running a palm over her hair to smooth it, she took a deep breath and forced a smile to her lips. She knew Gram would see right through it, but she had to try.

Head held high, she walked as quietly and serenely as possible into the bedroom. Gram sang softly to the baby, rocking slowly back and forth with Sammy tucked in the crook of her arm.

It was such a peaceful scene, and so much at variance with the frantic pace of Jasmine's heart, that she nearly turned tail and walked out again. But Gram caught her eye and smiled.

"He's sleeping soundly, dear," she said softly, continuing to rock. "I fed him the whole bottle. He's probably down for the count. Can you help me lay him in the bassinet?"

Jasmine nodded and moved forward, holding Sammy a moment longer than necessary, inhaling his sweet, baby scent and enjoying the feel of his soft skin against her cheek. It was only the threat of losing him that made her realize that she couldn't live without him.

It was more than just the schedule changes, the responsibility that came with having a newborn. More even than knowing there was someone completely dependent on her for his every need.

It was the space in her heart that grew larger every day, ebbing and flowing with love for this little one.

There was no way she was going to let Christopher take him away. She'd once thought the gaping hole he rent in her heart would never be mended. But loving Sammy forced her to open up her heart once again, to feel and live and hope.

She kissed the infant on his soft forehead and pushed the thatch of downy hair from his eyes. She wouldn't let the little guy down. No matter what.

"Is he gone?" Gram asked gently.

With an audible sigh, she took her grandmother's elbow and led her to the kitchen, where she seated the elderly woman on a foldout chair. Jenny's financial straits were obvious by the card table she used in place of a regular kitchen table.

Sammy had the best of everything, most of which had been bought by Jenny before her death. She had sacrificed everything for her unborn son, showing the kind of sweet, giving person she was all the way up to her last breath. She would have done anything for her Sammy.

Jasmine felt a tug of grief, and made a pretense of looking through the cupboard in order to have a moment to fold those feelings back into her memory. She already knew what was in the cupboards, which amounted to a box of peppermint tea and a box of saltine crackers.

"Do you want some tea?" she asked, hoping her voice didn't sound as high and squeaky to Gram as it did to her own ears. It annoyed her to betray her feelings in her voice, especially to Gram, who was already much too perceptive. With a determined effort, she steadied her voice and continued. "I think I'll have a cup, myself."

"Are you okay?"

She took her time pulling two mugs from a shelf and filling them with water, before turning to face her grandmother. "Yes, of course. Why wouldn't I be?"

"I can't imagine," Gram replied dryly.

She set the cups in the microwave and turned it on, then sat down across from her grandmother. "You're too wise for your own good."

Gram met Jasmine's gaze over the top of her spectacles and chuckled. "I haven't been alive for eighty years without learning something."

Jasmine reached for Gram's hand and squeezed it. "You've been so much help to me these past months," she admitted, her voice quavering with emotion. "I couldn't have made it without you."

"What's family for?" Gram said, waving off her comment with a slight grunt of protest.

The microwave buzzed, and Jasmine jumped up. As she dipped the tea bags into the mugs, she took a deep breath and plunged ahead. "It *was* Christopher at the door."

"Who else would it be? Didn't sound like he was in a hurry to leave, either."

"That's the understatement of the year," she agreed quietly. "I should have realized he'd be back, that he'd want to see Sammy at some point. I just wasn't prepared for him to show up today."

"And you sent him packing." It was a statement rather than a question, punctuated with a dry chuckle.

Jasmine laughed, but it didn't reach her heart. "You could say that. I slammed the door in his face."

"He'll be back." Gram nodded her head as if confirming her own words.

The flatness Jasmine felt when Christopher left wound itself more tightly around her chest. "I know," she whispered.

"What are you going to do about him?"

Gram was nothing if not direct, she reflected. No games. No beating around the bush. She just said what she thought and was done with it. One of the perks that came with age, Gram always said just before blurting out something outrageous.

Jasmine shook her head. "I don't know yet. Seeing him again confused me. I thought it would be easier. I thought..."

"That you hated him?" Gram queried gently, finishing the sentence for her. "Love doesn't give up so easily, my dear."

She shook her head fiercely. "No. I'm not in love with Christopher anymore." If her heart believed that, she wouldn't be quaking in her shoes, she thought acerbically. But she'd never admit it, not even to herself. "I've been over him for a long time."

"Have you?" Gram's questioning gaze met hers, and she looked away, afraid her grandmother would read the truth she knew must shine through her tears.

She couldn't love Christopher! Not after all these years, and especially not after everything he'd done to her and her family.

Then why did her heart leap when she saw him again?

She'd loved him since they were both in high school, she rationalized. For years they'd been inseparable. He'd been the man to whom she pledged her life, with whom she was ready to tie the knot.

Was it any wonder she would have such a polar reaction at seeing him again?

How could she not? It was only natural, after all, for her to have lingering feelings for a man who was such a large part of her past. Some of her happiest memories were with Christopher Jordan, and that was something his recent actions couldn't take away.

"My feelings don't matter," she said at last, shaking her head. "This isn't about me." She paused and took a deep breath, giving the bassinet a pointed look. "He wants to see Sammy. For all I know, he wants to take him away. And somehow, I've got to figure out a way to stop him."

Gram slowly stood and stretched, then shuffled to Jasmine's side, placing a consoling arm around her shoulders.

That the arm around her didn't have the power of former years mattered not a bit. Strength flowed from the elder to the younger with an intensity that only came from inner peace.

"I know this is hard for you, dear," she said, patting Jasmine's shoulder as she would to comfort a child. "But don't ignore your feelings. They are God given. Pray about it. Search your heart. And, Jasmine?"

"Mmm?"

"Talk to Christopher."

"*Talk* to him?" she screeched, her anger returning in spades. "Gram, I never thought *you'd* be on his side, after what happened to Jenny! Why should I *talk* to him?"

Gram's eyebrows creased as she frowned. "Don't you speak to me that way, young lady," she said, her tone brooking no argument. "I may be eighty, but I can still take you over my knee!"

Jasmine stepped back, surprised, then broke into a tired laugh, serving as a valve for the release of her anger. Gram was right, of course.

She hugged her grandmother as hard as the older woman's frail bones would allow. "I'm sorry," she said, her heart contrite. "I'm just confused. I'm sure I'll be all right after I pray about it." The words slipped out of her mouth from years of training, and she just wanted to bite her tongue. Pray about it, indeed.

Gram nodded, not appearing to notice the grimace Jasmine made. "I'll pray, too. It's the best we can do. The first thing, and the best. It'll all work out. In God's way, and in God's timing. We just have to look to Him and trust that He knows what's best."

Well, on that point, anyway, Jasmine couldn't agree more. God, if there was one, must certainly have something spectacular planned, or else He had a very peculiar sense of humor. If only she knew what He had in mind—and what role she was to play.

Christopher pulled a hard right off the gravel mountain road and drove into the brush, not caring that the pine trees were probably scratching the truck's exterior. When he was in far enough that he couldn't see the road, he slammed the gear into Park and shut down the engine.

This wasn't the way he'd meant it to be. He thumped a closed fist against the steering wheel. He hadn't meant to alienate Jasmine with the first words out of his mouth. What a big lug he was. Talk first, stick his big, dirty boots in his mouth afterward. He could certainly add his first encounter with her in a year to his ever-growing list of failures.

This one, however, he had to take full credit for. Much of what happened to him wasn't in his control, a part of God's will he couldn't understand. But this was completely his own doing, and he'd blown it big time. Not exactly a surprise, with his track record.

He'd been so certain he was meant to come back to Westcliffe. What else could he do? He loved Jasmine. He always had. To think of living without her—and Sammy—was unbearable.

But if his first encounter with her was anything to go by, he had a long way to travel to get back in her good graces. Her closed attitude left him shaken and unsure of himself. She didn't even try to hide how much she loathed seeing him again.

He lifted his hat and raked his fingers through the short ends of his hair. Frustration seethed through every nerve ending until his whole body tingled.

All he wanted to do was see Sammy, not run off with the boy like some criminal, though that's how he'd been treated. And Sammy had been in that bungalow. He'd heard the baby's cry and the soothing sounds of Jasmine's grandmother coming from the other room. What kind of a fool did she think he was?

The point of it—and that's what hurt—was that Jazz didn't want him to see the baby.

He understood her hesitance. He'd done a lot of things that needed explaining. But in the meantime, he'd hoped their years together would count for something.

He wasn't foolish enough to expect that he would be able to knock on her door and resume their relationship, where it had broken off before she'd gone off to med school, but couldn't she at least listen to him?

"Ha!" he said aloud, the sound echoing in the small cab of his truck. She hadn't listened to him then, and she wouldn't listen now.

Especially now. She wouldn't trust him any more than any other of Westcliffe's residents did. Far less, even, for she had more reasons to doubt him than the small town that virtually shunned his existence now that he was back.

The neighbors he could live without. Jasmine, he couldn't.

He'd hurt the woman he loved most in the world, and the knowledge sat like lead in his stomach. It was a burden he'd been carrying since the day she'd turned away from him and walked right out of his life. The day the world discovered he would soon be a father.

Jasmine thought he'd betrayed her, and mincing

words didn't change anything. Pain seared through his chest.

He wasn't denying his actions, no matter how questionable the whole thing was in his mind. What else could he have done, under the circumstances? He thought he was doing the right thing. He thought Jasmine would understand, that she'd want him to take the actions he'd decided on for Jenny's sake.

But she wouldn't even listen. What she'd learned, she hadn't learned from him, and he would regret that for the rest of his life. He should have made the trip to Denver as soon as he found out about Jenny. But there was so much to do, and not much time in which to do it.

He'd been so wrapped up in the tailspin his life had taken that he'd put it off, thinking he'd approach Jasmine when the ruckus had died down. After he'd taken care of the necessities, and before she'd heard the truth from someone else.

She still didn't know the truth. He'd hoped to tell her today.

He'd even hoped she'd forgive him. It was part of what drove him back to town—to ask her forgiveness for his part in the tragedy that had become their lives, and to ask for a second chance.

It was obviously not going to happen that way. He clamped his teeth together until he could feel his pulse pounding in his temples. What he wanted didn't matter. Not yet, and maybe not ever.

He had another responsibility—Sammy, the baby

he'd never seen. He wasn't going to let that boy down. And if that meant postponing the inevitable confrontation with Jasmine on personal issues, so be it.

His resolution did, however, present a unique set of circumstances, since he had to go through Jasmine to get to Sammy. Emotional issues aside, Jasmine was a formidable woman. If she decided to make things rough for him, there was no doubt in his mind she would succeed.

Which meant he had to convince her otherwise. Make her see reason. They needed to put the past aside, sit down together and discuss the issues like the adults they were.

This wasn't some high school spat they could just ignore and expect to go away. They were dealing with the welfare of a child. For all intents and purposes, *his* child.

His throat tightened. He had actually been relieved to hear Jasmine had been appointed Sammy's legal guardian, though he would never tell her so. He couldn't think of a better mother for the boy. He could depend on her to take care of Sammy as if he were her own.

And he could leave.

He recognized that the moment he'd seen the determination on Jasmine's face. He could turn around, walk right out of Westcliffe, and never look back, knowing Sammy was in capable hands. Loving hands.

And he would be doing no less than what everyone expected.

Maybe that would be best. How was he to know? He wasn't ready to be a father. What did he know about babies? He hadn't planned to be a father for a few years yet, after he and Jasmine had settled down. Blast it anyway, he didn't even know how to change a diaper.

What kind of hole had he dug for himself? And all because he was trying to do the right thing.

He blew out a breath and started the engine, gunning it into Reverse and making the wheels spin as he pulled back onto the dirt road. He shifted into gear and put the pedal to the metal.

Heading back toward town.

He couldn't leave. He couldn't go without Sammy, even knowing he was in Jasmine's capable hands. And though he knew he would cause a lot more pain before he could start mending hurts, it had to be done.

He had to go back. He needed Sammy in his life.

Sammy—and Jasmine.

Chapter Three

Three days later, Jasmine stared over the rim of her coffee cup at the soft-spoken cowboy across from her. The term *cowboy* used loosely, she thought wryly. Christopher had been born and raised in this mountain town, but he couldn't ride a horse to save his life. Ranching wasn't in his blood.

He looked the part, though, with his form-fitting western jeans, snap-down western shirt and a steel gray cowboy hat. Of course, he'd taken off the hat when he'd entered the café, exposing his thatch of windblown brown hair.

Another cowboy trait.

Her mind was being perversely obtuse this afternoon, she thought. How she could find anything humorous to laugh about in her present state of mind was beyond her comprehension. It was as if her subconscious were seeking to avoid the inevitable confrontation.

The determined gleam in Christopher's eyes and the hard set of his jaw gave him away. Why else would he have asked her to meet him in a small café in Wetmore, a half hour's drive from their home town and well out of the public eye?

She'd been surprised when he'd called yesterday and asked to meet her, but now she was as prepared as she'd ever be for whatever he would throw at her, though she still couldn't come up with a single acceptable reason for a man to abandon his wife and unborn child. And then return to claim his son after Jenny was dead. If he didn't want the boy before...

The familiar swell of anger rushed through her, but she tamped it down. She would listen. She owed him that much, whatever sort of torn and twisted man he'd become. He claimed he wanted Sammy, and today he would attempt to explain why.

Not that his words would make any difference. She already knew what her answer would be, despite anything he told her.

He couldn't have the baby. Not in a billion, trillion years.

Sammy was her son now. The papers declaring it so were firmly in her possession and valid in a court of law.

She'd fight him tooth and nail in court if she had to, but she prayed it wouldn't come to that. That was her true objective—to reason with him, to try to touch the man she once knew, the man buried deep inside the monster sitting across from her.

To make him leave quietly. And alone.

"What'll ya'll have?" said a waitress, tapping her pencil against her pad of paper. Her cheek near her bottom gum was plump with tobacco. Jasmine had heard of gum-chewing waitresses, but the thought of a tobacco-chewing waitress was more than her stomach could handle.

"A cup of hot tea for me," she said weakly, shifting her attention from the woman to focus on her queasy insides. "Peppermint, if you've got it."

She wasn't sure she could swallow even tea, but it occurred to her the peppermint might settle her stomach a little. She'd used it on Sammy's colic to good effect, so she could only hope it would ease some of her own distress.

"Double cheeseburger with everything, onion rings and a chocolate shake," Christopher ordered, smiling up at the waitress as if his entire life weren't hanging in the balance of this conversation.

Maybe it wasn't. Maybe he didn't care. Jasmine didn't know whether to feel relieved or annoyed.

It was obvious *his* appetite, at least, wasn't affected by their meeting. And *he* wasn't keeping his hands clenched in his lap to keep them from quivering, either. She pried her fingers apart and put her hands on the table.

Christopher cleared his throat and ran the tip of his index finger around the rim of his mug. "Remember when we used to sneak up here on Friday nights?'' he asked, chuckling lightly. His gaze met hers, the familiar twinkle in his light gray eyes making her heart skip a beat.

Jasmine felt her face warm under his scrutiny. She knew what he was thinking, the memories this café evoked. Two carefree youths, so much in love, their lives filled with laughter and happiness. And hope.

"We thought we were being so underhanded, slipping out of town.'' His light, tenor voice spread like silk over her. "Remember? We were so sure nobody noticed we were gone. We really thought we were pulling one over on everyone. And all the time, they were probably laughing and shaking their heads at us.''

Jasmine laughed quietly despite herself. "I'm sure Gram knew all along. She had such—'' She was going to say high hopes for the two of them, but the thought hit her like a slap in the face, so she left the end of her sentence dangling sharply in the air.

How ironic that he'd picked this location to meet today. She'd been so wrapped up in dealing with her crisis that she hadn't realized the poetic justice in his choosing this café. She swallowed hard, trying in vain to keep heat from suffusing her face.

It was the place where they'd first said *I love you.* The night they'd pledged themselves to each other forever. The night he'd asked her to be his wife. Before med school. And before Sammy.

She could see in his eyes that he was sharing her thoughts, reliving the memories right along with her. Her chest flooded with a tangle of emotions. Anger that he had brought her here. Hope because he remembered, too.

Had he brought her here on purpose, she wondered, as a way to have the upper hand? Or was this simply a convenient spot to meet, away from the prying eyes of the world? Did he mean to remind her of their joyful past, to taunt her with what could never be? She pinned him with her gaze, asking the question without speaking.

In answer, he swiped a hand down his face. "I'm sorry," he said, shaking his head regretfully. "It was thoughtless of me to bring us here. I should have realized—"

"It's okay," she interrupted, holding up a hand. "Better here than in Westcliffe, where we might be seen." She closed her eyes and eased the air from her lungs. At least he wasn't trying to rub her nose in the past, and for that, she was grateful.

He let out a breath that could have been a chuckle, but clearly wasn't, from the tortured look on his face. "I prayed about this meeting before I called you," he admitted in a low voice.

He clenched his napkin in his fist and looked out the window, allowing Jasmine to study his chiseled profile. There were small lines around his eyes, and dark furrows on his forehead. They weren't laugh lines, she noticed sadly. He looked ten years older than his twenty-eight years.

"Truth be told," he continued, still avoiding her eyes, "praying is about the only thing I've been doing for weeks."

His admission wasn't what she expected, and it took her aback. She remained silent for a moment, trying to digest what he was telling her.

She'd assumed from his actions that he'd played his faith false, that he'd given up on God and was taking his own way with things.

Abandoning his family was hardly the act of a man walking with his Maker. But now he was telling her, in so many words, that his faith was still intact. That he believed God was in control. That he believed prayer would help this wretched situation. That God was *here.*

She barely restrained the bitter laugh that desperately wanted to escape her lips. Irony seethed through her. How had he kept his faith in God when hers so easily disappeared?

He smiled, almost shyly, as if his revelation had taken great effort. It probably had, though there was a time when there had been nothing they couldn't share between them.

In so many ways, she wanted to close her eyes, embrace his belief, wipe the slate clean and start all over again. To return to the time in her life when she believed, and when her belief had given her hope.

But that was naiveté. She wasn't a child, to believe in miracles. To believe in a close, personal God who would help her through life's problems. Her faith was ebbing and flowing like waves on rocks.

She wasn't even sure she believed in God, at least in a personal God who watched over His flock like a shepherd watching over His sheep.

She couldn't—and didn't—pay Him more than lip service, and at this point she was hardly doing that. Although she hadn't denied her faith outright, she hadn't set foot in a church in months.

The subject humiliated and frustrated her. All those years she considered her faith strong, yet it wilted with the first attack of trial.

Some Christian she was. Or maybe she never had been. She was too confused to know.

How could she believe in a God who would allow Christopher to get away with what he'd done?

And Jenny—what about Jenny? If God was there, why hadn't He helped her? Why hadn't He healed her? He'd forced Jasmine to stand helpless and watch her sister die, her head crammed full of medical knowledge and unable to do a thing to save her.

"Would you pray with me?" he asked when she didn't answer.

Prayer. Gram suggested it before, and now Christopher was bringing up the issue. Her heart clenched. It wasn't as if she never tried.

She had. Last night on her knees beside her bed.

But the words wouldn't come, and the space between her and the heavenly realm seemed unbridgeable. God wasn't listening. Or He had cut her off. As she had once cut off Christopher.

She shook her head. "We're in a public restaurant, Christopher. Let's just get down to business."

She cringed inside as she said the words. It wasn't *business*. It was a baby's life they were talking about.

He looked vaguely astonished, but he didn't argue. Instead, his gentle smile tipped the corner of his lips as he reached for her hand, which she quickly snatched from his grasp.

Shrugging, he plunged into the reason they were meeting. "You know what I want. I want to see Sammy. I want to—"

"Take him away from me?" she snapped, heedless of the fact that she hadn't given him a chance to finish his sentence. Suddenly she felt completely unsure of herself as Sammy's guardian, of her ability to provide what he needed. Without thinking, she took her insecurity out on the man sitting across from her. "I don't think so, Christopher."

He opened his mouth to protest, but she gestured for him to stop.

"You need to understand something," she continued, her voice crackling with intensity. "You weren't around when Sammy was born. You didn't walk him up and down the hall at all hours of the night because he had colic and didn't want to sleep. You haven't changed him, fed him or bathed him."

"I haven't even—"

She pinned him with a glare. "I have. *I* was the one there for Sammy. And *I* am going to be the one to raise him."

"But I want—" His voice closed around the words and he coughed. "I want to do all those things. I want to be there for the boy. My..." He hesitated. "My son."

He looked petulant, and his eyes pleaded for her mercy.

Why, oh why did his mere physical presence affect her so? He once used those very same big blue-gray eyes to get his own way with her when they argued over which movie to see or where to go for dinner.

This wasn't one of those times. Nor was it a debatable issue.

"Let me explain something to you," she said, her voice splintering with restrained anger. "I very frankly don't give a snip what your story is. I don't even want to hear it, though I'm sure you've spent many hours rehearsing for my benefit."

His scowl darkened and he grunted in protest.

"No, really. It doesn't matter. Nothing you say matters. What *matters* is that I've bonded with this baby, and nothing is going to convince me to give him away. Most especially to you."

With a sharp intake of breath, he sat back in his

seat and pounded a fist on the tabletop, making the silverware rattle.

Water from her cup splashed onto the surface of the table, and she quickly wiped it with the edge of her napkin, her face flaming with anger and embarrassment. She hazarded a glance at the neighboring booths, wondering if anyone had noticed his outburst.

"Even before you've heard what really happened?" he asked through clenched teeth, his chest rising and falling with the exertion of each angry breath.

She lifted one sardonic brow. "Astonish me. You were abducted by aliens. You've been in a coma. You had amnesia. What, Christopher? What's your story?" As much as she tried to keep her voice low, it lifted with each word to a higher crescendo until she'd reached well beyond shrill and piercing.

Now *she* was the one causing the scene, and it was *his* fault. She didn't care how irrational and childish the thought was. She clamped her jaw shut and glared defiantly at Christopher, and then at the patrons staring at her. Life had freeze-framed, with everyone's attention on her.

She blew out a frustrated breath, furious that he had provoked her to make a display of herself.

"Jazz," he began, reaching out with both hands in a conciliatory gesture.

She threw her napkin down on the table and stood. "I thought this meeting was a good idea when you first suggested it," she said slowly, articulating each syllable in a low, precise tone. "I was mistaken."

She looked blindly out the window, then back to Christopher. "I love Sammy, and he's staying with me. End of subject." She met his gaze briefly, willing her strength to hold out until she could flee from his presence. "Goodbye, Christopher."

She turned and walked away from him, holding her chin high and staying steadfastly determined not to look at the patrons she felt were staring at her.

Christopher could pick up the tab on the check. It served him right. Her blood boiling, she wished momentarily that she'd ordered a full-course steak dinner instead of just hot tea.

When she exited the café, she pulled in a deep breath of mountain air, closing her eyes as fresh, cool oxygen flooded her lungs. If only she could dissipate the heat in her brain as easily.

Walking away from Christopher was the hardest thing she'd ever done. He was suffering in his own way, she realized, and her presence affected him as much as his did her.

All the more reason for them to stay away from each other, she decided, fortifying her decision with every justification available to her.

Her heart said a father should be with his son. Her mind said Christopher forfeited that right when he walked away from Jenny and his unborn baby.

She had to cling to reason, no matter what her

emotions were doing. Sammy's well-being depended on it. Probably her own happiness, too. She loved that baby. And for now, maybe for always, that love would have to be enough.

Christopher ate his food in silence, ignoring the curious stares and speculative talk around him. His mind was so preoccupied with his troubles that he barely tasted his food, and had to order a second milk shake to wash the hamburger down his dry throat.

He loved Jasmine more than ever. He thought the feelings had faded some with time, but sitting across from her today, he knew he was fooling himself. The ache in his chest only shaded his deeper feelings. He would do anything to wipe the pain from her eyes, and it was the ultimate irony to know he'd been the one to put it there in the first place. Sure, Jasmine was being harsh and stubborn, but who could blame her? He knew it was her fear of losing Sammy that was speaking for her. She'd always been an all-or-nothing kind of woman, a fact Christopher admired. Her obvious devotion and loyalty to her nephew only made him love her more.

Pain lanced his temple, and he reached a hand up to rub it firmly across his brow. Nothing was going as he had hoped.

He knew without a doubt that when she walked away today, she wouldn't meet with him again, at least not intentionally. She'd run the other direction whenever she saw him, screaming inwardly if not in reality.

Which meant his next move must be furtive. He'd have to follow her around until an opportunity presented itself to speak with her again—in a time and in a location where she had no place to go except into his arms.

God would give him that opportunity. Or maybe he'd have to make his own.

Jasmine didn't immediately return to Gram's apartment, where she was staying with Sammy. She knew Gram would take care of the baby as long as necessary. And right now, Jasmine needed to be alone, to have time to think.

Not entirely conscious of where she was going or why, she found herself parking in front of Jenny's cottage. There was still a lot of work to be done, she supposed. And it was quiet here, a far cry from the hustle and bustle of the medical clinic.

Once in the small cabin, she started to absently box up Jenny's things, beginning with the books in her room. She picked up an empty apple box from the pile and began stacking various romance novels spine up, mixed with some hardbacked classic literature.

Jasmine laughed to herself, trying to picture her flighty sister reading the classics. Fashion magazines were more her style.

Had been her style. Jasmine quickly sobered.

How well had she really known Jenny? She suspected not as well as she should have, especially in the last few years.

They'd been close as children, though there was four years difference between them. But they had drifted apart when Jasmine reached high school and got interested in friends, makeup and boys.

In Christopher.

And when Jenny caught up, she'd taken a different road than Jasmine, who'd been class president and received straight A's. Jenny hung out with the flashy crowd, the ones with too much money and too much time. Jasmine had always wondered what Jenny could have in common with her friends.

She didn't have money, and she wasn't college-bound. She just didn't seem the type. But she appeared to be happy, and Jasmine had left it alone. How she'd ended up with a simple cowboy like Christopher was beyond Jasmine.

And then she'd gone off to college herself, thanks to the grant from the city, increasing the emotional distance between the two sisters. As far as she knew, Jenny had grown into a beautiful, self-assured adult, a relative stranger she greeted with a kiss on the cheek when she came home from the holidays. Had Jenny been seeing Christopher even then?

There was always laughter in the house during vacations and holidays. Jasmine puckered her brow, straining to remember if her sister had been part of the joyous festivities. Or had she been off with friends? Jasmine couldn't remember. Probably, she'd been too busy with Christopher to notice, a thought which gave her a guilty start.

Shaking her head to clear her introspection, Jasmine carried the box of books into the living room, where the rest of Jenny's boxed goods were stored, and went to Jenny's room to begin stripping the bedclothes. Her sister's sweet, airy scent still lingered on the sheets, and she brought a pillow to her face, inhaling deeply.

"We never said goodbye," she whispered aloud, hugging the pillow to her chest. She wished she had one more minute, just one, to give Jenny a hug and tell her how much she was loved.

Jasmine shook herself from her melancholy with some effort. Funny how grief hit her at the oddest moments. She'd think her emotions were under control, and then in a second's time, grief would wash over her and overwhelm her, sometimes for no apparent reason.

Those were the toughest times, the moments before she found the strength to tuck her grief back away and go on living, because that's what she had to do. Because she was here and Jenny was not, and baby Sammy depended on her.

She reached for the other pillow, but when she yanked at the corner to pull off the pillowcase, Jenny's Bible fell to the floor.

Jasmine had forgotten all about it. She'd slipped it under the pillow when Christopher had shown up.

She was relieved to find it now. It was a part of Jenny she wanted to keep.

Heart in her throat, she reached down and scooped it up, tenderly smoothing the bent pages before closing the cracked leather. Sitting on the stripped bed with one leg tucked under her, she ran a hand across the front of the Bible, considering whether it would be right to read more of the notes Jenny had written in the margins.

She was so confused, so hurt. And she missed her sister terribly. Would it be a breach of trust to read a little, to bring Jenny near through her words, her thoughts and dreams and faith? Who knew but that maybe, in some small way, it would help her know what to do about Christopher and Sammy.

She could only hope for such a miracle, even if she didn't believe in miracles anymore.

Chapter Four

The next morning, Christopher eyed the two-room log cabin, turning over the possibilities in his mind. After leaving the diner, he'd phoned an old high school football buddy, who'd lent him this place for the weekend. If God was willing and he planned right, it would be his and Jasmine's for at least one completely uninterrupted, if not happy, day.

Loose gravel and pine needles crunched under his feet as he approached the cabin, his friend's fishing hideaway. Nothing spectacular—it didn't even have electric heat. But for what Christopher had in mind, it was perfect.

He'd purposely picked a cabin tucked up just far enough into the Sangre de Cristo mountain range to keep the clinic from sending in emergency equipment right away, yet far enough from town to warrant Jasmine's personal attention.

Not to mention high enough in altitude to get a good snow, if the weather cooperated.

He eyed the sky critically, wondering when the snow would start. The weather forecast indicated a major storm heading their way. It could snow five feet in a day here, given the right conditions.

He only hoped these *were* the right conditions, external and internal. And that Jasmine would come when he called, even if she knew about the impending snowstorm. If they sent a couple of paramedics from Wetmore after him, he was in a world of hurt.

He laughed despite his sour mood.

She would come. Jasmine Enderlin was the singularly most compassionate woman he'd ever known. She wouldn't give a second's thought to risking her own life and health in order to help someone who needed her, a quality that made her a terrific doctor and an even better person.

His respect for her was only superseded by his love.

If he could just blurt out the truth of the past and wipe the slate clean, things would be much simpler. *If* she would listen. *If* she would believe him.

And *if* he had only himself to consider. He wouldn't waste a second before telling her everything. And he sure wouldn't be at 9500 feet constructing ridiculous undercover adventures better suited to spy novels than to an old-fashioned man who couldn't give up his dreams.

But right now he'd do just about anything—including spy novel antics, in order to see her again.

Again he glanced at the sky, wondering how long he had left to prepare. He had wood to chop, dinner to make and a leg to break.

He chuckled softly at his own joke, then quickly sobered, drawing in a breath, clenching his jaw and pressing his lips together as he determinedly went to find an ax.

I married Christopher tonight. Mrs. Christopher Jordan. Jenny Jordan. How awkward that sounds!

I still can't believe things worked out the way they did. Everything seemed so hopeless, and then there was Christopher and...

He gave me a rose at the altar. A single, beautiful white rose. I've pressed it into this Bible as a keepsake—the only one I really have of my wedding day.

It all happened so fast. No photographer. No wedding cake. No guests. Except for Gram, who stood up for me, and Christopher's brother from Texas, his only living relative, for him. Jasmine was there in the back, but she didn't say anything.

Jasmine cringed inwardly. She'd only gone because she thought it would be spineless not to. And she wanted to show them she was bigger than that.

Oh, she was bigger, all right. Pouting in the back and glaring at everyone. She'd never even wished the couple happiness.

She shook herself from her thoughts and continued reading, picking up where she'd left off.

But at least I can keep this rose. I know what he was trying to communicate with a white rose rather than a red one. He doesn't love me. He loves Jasmine, and he always has.

But he's committed himself to me, now. Me and my baby. And Christopher is an honorable man. He won't go back on his word.

I hope, in time, he'll learn to love me, though I know it will never be the kind of love he has for Jasmine. But no matter how he feels about me, he'll love the baby. And he'll be a good daddy. If there was ever a man who was meant to be a father, it's Christopher.

Jasmine barely restrained herself from crumpling the piece of paper in her hands. She'd found it tucked into the page with the family tree, where Jenny had carefully written hers and Christopher's names on the appropriate lines. She'd drawn a heart where their baby's name would go.

She tucked the paper deep into the binding and closed the Bible with a pop. Her throat constricted until no air could pass through, but it didn't matter. She wasn't breathing anyway. Constrained air lodged squarely in her chest, throbbing mercilessly against her rib cage.

Christopher still loved her, even when he married Jenny? Oh, sure, but Jenny was carrying his child.

She was more confused now than ever. Nothing Jenny had written made sense! She stared at the Bible for a moment, then tossed it away with a frustrated groan.

Jasmine nearly launched herself off the bed at the sound of her pager. Placing a palm to her chest to slow her rapidly beating heart, she reached her other hand for her pager and turned it off.

The sweet strength of adrenaline pumped through her, clearing her head. While she wasn't like some of the residents she'd linked up with when she was in Denver, to whom the excitement of the moment was their reason to serve, she couldn't deny the pulse-pounding anticipation of being needed. It thrilled her to have something to give back to the little town that had given her so much.

She reached the phone and dialed the clinic number. Jill, the county nurse, gave Jasmine a quick rundown. A man had called from a mountain cabin just above Horn Lake. He'd been fishing, apparently, when he slipped off a wet log and fell.

"He's all alone, and he's afraid to drive. And Jasmine—he says he doesn't have insurance and can't afford a hospital. Or a doctor."

Jasmine made a noise from the back of her throat

that signaled her compassionate understanding of his situation.

She pictured a gray-haired widower finding solace fishing in a mountain lake, afraid even to call the clinic because of the expense. An old man, all alone, with a broken leg and no one to help him.

The picture in her mind was too much for her heart to take. She'd work for free if she must, knowing that her actions would open a whole other can of worms should she be discovered dispensing her charity.

"What are the coordinates?" she asked, balancing a pad of paper on her hip so she could write them down.

Jill gave her the exact location of the cabin, someone renting the old Wallaby place. Then she paused expectantly.

"I'm going up there," Jasmine said, answering Jill's unspoken question. She reached into her jeans pocket for the keys to her four-by-four. "I have my bag with me. As long as it's not too major, I can handle a broken leg on my own. If it's too bad, I'll drive him back to the clinic myself. An ambulance crew wouldn't want to hike up into the lake area anyway."

"It's starting to snow, Jazz. The weather forecast says we might be in for a blizzard," Jill warned. "You never know how bad it's going to be. Maybe you ought to let Wetmore's EMT take care of it."

There was more than one EMT, and they were all

men. Jill didn't have to say it for it to be true. And she was probably right.

But this was Jasmine's call, and an inner prompting was telling her to go.

"No, it's okay. I can get there faster. The poor old guy is probably in a lot of pain." And it would give her something to do to keep her mind off Christopher and her problems, she added silently. "I have my cell phone. If I have any problems, I'll give the guys in Wetmore a ring. I promise."

"Jazz, I didn't say—" Jill began, but Jasmine didn't let her finish as she put down the phone and raced to her car. Checking her sports utility vehicle for gas and equipment, she quickly got on the road. It took her half an hour to drive the dirt road as far as it ran toward Horn Lake.

When she reached the end of the line, she pulled her parka snug around her chin, gathered her gear onto her backpack, and began the hike up to the lake. A breeze had picked up, stinging her cheeks with bitter cold. Gritting her teeth, she ignored the icy pain and concentrated on putting one foot in front of another.

Just when she was getting to where she was no longer able to ignore the cold, she spied the cabin she was seeking. It was a run-down old place, more of a summer home than a winter hideaway. Jasmine wondered at the old man living in such conditions year-round.

Could a broken heart cause such misery? Her own

heart clenched, answering the question on its own. Jasmine knew too well the feeling of abandonment, and she prayed she'd be able to help this neighbor, whoever he was, in more ways that one.

It occurred to her then that she hadn't asked for her patient's name, a major oversight not like her to make. Maybe those short nights *were* getting to her.

Her mind had been preoccupied, trying *not* to think about Christopher, she reminded herself, knocking firmly on the door. When no one answered, she tried again. And again.

Finally, she pounded on the door with her fist, wondering if her patient had been hurt worse than she'd first imagined. "Hello? Is anyone in there? Can you hear me?"

She'd break the door down if she had to, but it occurred to her to try the handle first. It turned easily in her palm and the catch switched, making the door swing inward. Jasmine shivered and swallowed hard. It was odd for the door to be unlocked.

She ignored the uncomfortable feeling of a stranger making herself welcome and stepped inside the cabin. "Hello? I knocked, but no one answered! Sir? Are you here?"

The scene inside the cabin was anything but frightening. In fact, if she didn't know better, she would think it was the setting of a lovers' secret rendezvous.

The only light came from a fire crackling in the old stone hearth. It basked the room in a soft, flickering glow similar to candlelight, but with the sharp, pungent scent of pine. The wooden floor had been recently swept, and firewood was stacked neatly in one corner.

A meal was set on a checkered cloth on an old, rickety table whose spindly legs looked like they might collapse at any moment. A tingle went up her spine as she realized the meal was set for *two*.

Clearly, she was not the one expected in this cabin. Her first thought was that she'd made a mistake, gotten the coordinates wrong and entered someone else's cabin.

But that couldn't be. This was the old Wallaby place, though others owned it now. It was too hard to keep track of all the summer residents who came and went. She struggled to remember who might have rented the cabin after Grace and Chuck Wallaby moved to Arizona.

Suddenly she noticed that the rocking chair facing the fire was slowly tipping back and forth without so much as a squeak to give it away.

Someone was in the cabin. But why didn't he answer when she called?

She tensed, then forced herself to relax. Fear and mortification warred within her for prominence. There was no reason for her to feel embarrassed, necessarily, but heat flamed her cheeks nonetheless.

She was a doctor responding to a call, she reminded herself sternly, taking a deep breath and squaring her shoulders. His broken leg might not be much, if he was rocking in a chair with that pain, but his hearing left a lot to be desired.

"Excuse me," she said loudly enough to cause an echo. She moved into the firelight, wanting to see and be seen. She didn't want the poor guy to think she was sneaking up on him. "I guess you didn't hear me knock. I'm Dr. Enderlin, and I've come to see about your—"

She paused, the breath cut off from her throat, as her eyes met a warm blue-gray gaze and her heart slammed into her rib cage.

"Christopher!"

"I see you made it," Christopher said, tipping his head toward her in greeting. "I was going to go looking for you if you didn't show up soon."

He neglected to mention that it had taken all the force of his will not to bolt into the winter chill to search for her when she didn't arrive as quickly as he'd expected. Only knowing he'd ruin any chance of convincing her to stay and listen if she discovered his scheme too soon kept him glued to his chair and praying for her safety.

Night came swiftly onto the mountains. Horn Peak quickly blocked out the feeble rays of the winter sun as it set for the night. It would be dark in a matter of minutes.

Her cheeks, already flushed a pleasant pink, rose in color, contrasting starkly with the silky weave of her sable hair. Her mouth opened briefly before she clamped it shut again and stood arms akimbo, a glare marring the sheer beauty of her face.

"You're angry," he said aloud, realizing as he spoke that he was stating the obvious.

She made a pointed glance down one of his legs, which were crossed loosely at the ankles, and up the other one before coming to rest back on his face. Her gaze made his skin tingle all over, and he shifted in his seat like a man with poison ivy.

Guilt tugged at his chest, and he shrugged at her unspoken question. When she looked back at his wool sock-encased feet, he chuckled and wiggled his toes.

"Please tell me you didn't call me up here on a ruse," she said, her voice hoarse, whether from restrained emotion or from her walk in the chill night air, he couldn't say.

He cleared his throat, struggling between feeling mildly guilty and very self-satisfied. She was up here, wasn't she? Even if she *had* come under false pretenses, his intentions were good.

"Well...if you mean do I have a broken leg, then I guess the answer would have to be no," he drawled, tipping up the corner of his lip in a half smile he hoped would endear himself to her and not further raise her ire. He wasn't nearly as cocky as he used to be about the easy cowboy charm that had always worked with Jasmine.

"I see," she said, swinging her backpack off her back and holding it in front of her like a shield. Her fists clenched the material, her knuckles white. Christopher flinched inwardly, offering a silent prayer for the right words to say. Why did it have to be like this between them, when it used to be so good?

"I didn't call you up here on a ruse," he denied flatly.

"Really? Then what *do* you call it?"

"Embellishment. I stretched the truth a little because we need to talk."

"A little?" One eyebrow rose as she glared at both of his perfectly sturdy legs. "I drop everything to make a risky call in the middle of a major snowstorm, and you say you exaggerated a *little?*"

"If it makes you feel any better, I think I sprained my ankle chopping wood for the fire."

Her eyes were glowing, and he knew her well enough to know she was holding back a smile. But he could tell she was still harboring her irritation and resentment, and with good reason, he had to admit.

"I'd never do anything to hurt you, Jazz. Five more minutes and I would have come after you. I'd never put you in danger or let you get hurt, not when it's in my power to protect you."

"How comforting," she said dryly, turning away from him and surveying the room. "A knight in shining armor who tosses his damsel in distress to the dragon before attempting to save her." She turned back and smoothed a hand down her hair, which was attractively disheveled by the hood of her parka. "Does this place have a phone I can use?"

"Of course. On the far wall, next to the table."

Shedding her coat, she walked over to the antique phone and dialed a number, talking in hushed tones to the person on the other end of the line.

Christopher watched, a smile playing on his lips, as she picked at the cheese, crackers and fruit on the table as she talked. Things were working out far better than he'd anticipated. He half figured he'd have to hog-tie her to get her to stay with him, and here she was taking off her coat and eating the food he prepared for her all of her own volition.

Perhaps she knew how critical it was that the two of them worked things out. He was the first to admit it would take far more than a good talk to untangle this mess. But it was a start.

And afterward, he was prepared to follow up those words with action, to slay her dragons and bring her home to safety. Jasmine—and Sammy, too.

He wondered if she noticed the bouquet of red roses lying next to the bottle of sparkling cider. And if she did notice, would she realize the flowers were for her? Hope swelled in his chest and he swallowed hard.

He sat back in the rocking chair, giving her privacy to finish her conversation. She was probably calling Gram about Sammy, and he didn't want to pressure her.

She hung up the phone and went to stand by the fire, holding her hands palms out toward the flames. It was all Christopher could do not to join her at the hearth, wrap his arms around her tiny waist and bury his face in her long, soft hair.

It was something he would have done, in the past. They would have stared at the fire and talked in hushed tones about their future, reaffirming with every look and caress the strength of the love that passed between them.

It was like being run through with a bull's horn not to be able to hold her now. He stopped rocking, holding his breath through the endless moment of silence.

Finally, she turned and met his gaze, her dark eyes warm with emotion and the glow of the fire. "I want you to know that I'm just warming up here by the fire for a few minutes before I head back to my truck. I'm not staying, if that's what you're thinking."

"Jazz, you can't just turn around and walk out of here!" he began, but she cut him off when he tried to continue.

"I made it up here just fine, and the hike is downhill from here." She blew out a breath. "I can't stay, Christopher. Please. Don't try to make me."

The spur in his gut raked his insides like a cowboy's heels on a bucking bronc.

She wet her bottom lip with the tip of her tongue

and continued. "Since it appears there's no medical emergency, I'm needed in town."

"I didn't call you up here to be a doctor, Jasmine, no matter what I said to the nurse on the phone."

She paused and breathed heavily, as if testing her words in her head before speaking them aloud. "I know," she said, her voice a low purr. "And I think I understand."

"Then stay."

She shook her head. "I appreciate what you're trying to do here, but—"

He would have interrupted her again, but her pager beat him to it.

Jasmine turned the blaring instrument off and glanced at the number. "I need to use your phone again," she said, her voice dull.

"Go ahead."

He rose and stood behind her as she made contact with the clinic in town. This conversation he wanted to hear, and he didn't think she'd mind his eavesdropping.

"Doctor Enderlin here," she began, then stiffened. "What?" Her voice went unnaturally shrill, sending a shudder of premonition through Christopher.

He reached out with a tentative hand and withdrew it again twice before finally laying a gentle palm on her shoulder. She tensed for a moment, then eased back into the stronghold of his arms. It only seemed natural to wrap his arm around the front of her shoulders in a move that was equally firm and gentle.

A silent offering to lend her strength. Her whole body quivered beneath his touch, and he knew it was the voice on the other end of the line that was making her shake.

And it wasn't good news.

"Forward her call to me," she said in a pinched voice. As she waited, she pulled a notepad and pen from her breast pocket, scribbling madly when the voice on the other end of the line resumed. She paused every so often to ask a question or clarify a response, but through it all, her trembling increased.

Moments later, she hung up and redialed the clinic. She put her notepad down and plastered her grip on his forearm, her gaze seeking his for reassurance. He gave her everything he had, tightening his hold just enough to let her know he read the terror in her eyes. And to let her know he was there for her, no matter what.

He watched in amazement as the doctor in Jasmine surfaced, masking the fear. Her features composed and relaxed and a determined gleam lit her eyes. So complete was the transformation that Christopher wondered if he hadn't imagined her alarm.

She squared her shoulders, which he took as a cue to drop his arm from around her and step back. "No, his leg wasn't broken. Minor *sprain,*" she said, tossing him a glance that made him cringe. "I've already taken care of it."

No you haven't, he disagreed mentally. *We haven't even started.*

But if someone needed her medical attention, she'd leave. And he'd let her go, of course. Shoot, he'd go with her.

"I'm only a ten-minute hike at most from that cabin. I can reach her."

A ten-minute hike. In this weather? Ten minutes would seem like an hour. He picked up her parka. It was soaking wet. He moved it close to the fire, knowing it wouldn't have time to dry before she left. And a damp coat would make that hike every bit more excruciating.

"Who's injured?" he asked when she hung up the phone. She drew a breath and pinned him with her gaze.

"Not injured. Amanda Carmichael is stranded alone in her cabin, and she's having her baby. *Now.*"

He didn't miss the fear that briefly flashed in her eyes. Was she remembering Jenny's death?

He muttered a prayer for her comfort under his breath, and steeled himself to do what he could to answer that prayer on his own. If all he could do was stand by her and support her, then that's what he would do. And he might even surprise her.

His mind clicked into gear, reviewing the things he had learned. During the last year away from Westcliffe, God had given him the opportunity to prove himself as well as to help people in need.

The Carmichaels lived a short distance away, thank God. "We'll use the snowmobile," he said, thinking aloud.

"What?" she said, looking confused.

"I'm going with you."

Chapter Five

‹‹There's no need," Jasmine said. The words were so firm and frosty they would have rivaled the air outside, but he wouldn't be moved from his purpose.

"I know there's no need. I *want* to help."

"You'll just be in the way."

"Maybe," he agreed, reaching for her parka and wrapping it around her, wincing at how cold and damp it still felt. "But I'm going anyway."

Jasmine met his gaze square on. Probing. Testing. He held perfectly still, barely breathing as he let her see inside his heart.

After a moment, she shrugged and turned away from him. "Whatever. But I'm leaving now."

Christopher snatched his own coat from a rack near the door and quickly zipped it up. "It'll only take me a minute to warm up my snowmobile." He planted his cowboy hat on his head by the crown and straightened the brim with his fingers.

"Good idea. We'll get there in half the time. I'll wait," she said, looking as if she weren't very happy about it but was determined to follow through.

Christopher warmed up the engine, then went back inside the cabin to get Jasmine, who was by this time pacing the floor. He hid a smile. She never had been the patient type. Probably why she was a doctor.

Ugh. He shook his head. His puns were getting worse by the moment. Could stress do that to a person? The thought nearly made him chuckle, if he wasn't so cold and the situation so serious. "Bundle up, darlin'. It's a raging blizzard out there, and we're heading right smack into it."

He wasn't kidding, Jasmine thought as she mounted the snowmobile behind Christopher. It was freezing and then some. The wind was blowing so fiercely the falling snow was almost horizontal to the ground.

"Hang on tight!" he yelled over the wind, and Jasmine tentatively wrapped her arms around his waist. It was funny how an action could be at once so awkward and yet so disturbingly familiar.

She clung tightly to him as the vehicle bounded over the snow toward the Carmichaels' cabin. In the brief conversation she'd had with Amanda, she was reassured that the labor was progressing along normally, if quickly.

Amanda was certain she would have the baby any moment. Unusual to have such a short labor with a first baby, but Jasmine had seen odder wonders in her time at the hospital in Denver. The best and the worst.

She swallowed hard and squeezed her eyes shut, trying not to think about Jenny. Trying not to think about death, when she should be concentrating on welcoming a new life into the world.

There was nothing to worry about, she reassured herself, praying all the while God would make it so. She'd spent her requisite time on the maternity ward during her residency. She knew how to deliver a baby. She had all the necessary equipment, unless there was a problem, in which case she'd call for a back up.

She'd known coming back to Westcliffe that, while most expectant mothers made it to the hospital in Pueblo for their labor and delivery, she would be called on from time to time to deliver a baby.

And she'd had confidence in her baby-delivering skills until Jenny died. Watching her sister hemorrhage and knowing she was powerless to stop it was nearly the end of her medical career, never mind the permanent scars it left on her heart.

She knew how irrational it sounded. Jenny's death didn't have anything to do with delivering Sammy. But that didn't stop Jasmine from remembering, and the memory made her shaky.

It had taken all her effort to continue serving as

the doctor to the town, and it was only her sense of obligation to its people that kept her there now.

What she really wanted to do was run away, hide her head in the sand like an ostrich. Now more than ever. How could she help Amanda and act as if nothing troubled her?

She could, and she would. She clenched her teeth together and concentrated on reigning in the strong wash of emotion coursing through her.

She was a doctor. Doctors sometimes lost patients, and it wasn't their fault. If she internalized guilt every time something went wrong that was beyond her control, she would go crazy.

But Jenny wasn't just any patient, and Jasmine couldn't just lightly brush it away. The knowledge that she might not be able to help Amanda Carmichael shook her to the core. Women died in childbirth, even in the twentieth century. The shiver that coursed through her had nothing to do with the cold.

Christopher took one hand away from the handlebar and placed it over her clutched fingers. She leaned her cheek into the strength of his back and sighed. It felt good to be in his company again. Good, natural and right, as if she'd never left.

And despite the offhand manner in which she'd answered him back at the cabin, she needed him now. Desperately. She needed his strength and assurance, and most especially his faith.

He pulled the snowmobile up to the front of the house, a small, A-frame log cabin similar to the one from which they'd come. Modest, but made for the weather, the building was a solid fixture against the raging of the storm.

Christopher removed the key and dismounted in record time. He held his gloved hand out to her, his lips pressed together grimly.

By the look on his face, Jasmine couldn't tell if he was angry or worried. Maybe a little of both. But she knew him well enough to know he'd put his own feelings aside long enough to help another human being out of a jam. Even if she was that person. And Amanda, of course. He would ignore the tension between them for Amanda's sake, as well as the baby's.

He saw her face and flashed her an encouraging smile. Reassured, she reached for his hand.

She expected him to release her fingers when she was free of the machine, but instead he tucked her hand under his arm and gave it a reassuring squeeze. ''I'm here for you, Jasmine,'' he whispered gruffly, then gave the thick oak door a solid knock.

It wasn't likely Amanda would hear them knocking over the wind, so she wasn't surprised when no one answered. Christopher knocked again, then looked to her for guidance.

She stepped forward and tried the doorknob, which moved easily in her hand. ''Amanda?'' she called, stepping into the cabin out of the snow and wind, noting that Christopher followed her in. She heard a muffled cry from the back of the cabin and gestured for him to sit while she found Amanda, who was in the back bedroom, looking tired and peaked. Her pale green eyes gleamed with a mixture of anxiety and excitement. Her short, curly auburn hair was stuck to her forehead where streaks of sweat had dried, and the freckles that marked her face became more pronounced with her pallor. Her small frame looked thin and skeletal, except for the pronounced bulge of her abdomen.

She was a small woman, like Jenny. Small women sometimes had more trouble delivering. Jasmine cut off the thought before it could reach its completion.

"Dr. Enderlin!" she exclaimed, attempting weakly to sit up on the bed. "I'm so glad you're here! My water broke, and these contractions hit me real hard! I thought I was going to be popping this kid out all by my lonesome!"

"Well, that isn't going to happen," Jasmine replied, laying a comforting hand on her arm. "We're here now. Lie back on the bed and rest while you can. You're going to need all your energy for pushing."

Amanda nodded.

"Do you know Christopher Jordan?" she asked, her voice clipped with the calm, emotionless demeanor she used with her patients.

"Sure."

"He's here to lend me a hand. Is that okay with you?"

"I don't care who helps," she said sharply, curling into herself as another contraction hit. "Just get this baby out of me!"

Jasmine ignored Amanda's terse words, knowing it was pain speaking and not the voice of her neighbor. "I'll be right back with Christopher, and we'll see what we can do about getting you out of pain and introducing you to your new little one."

As she went back to get Christopher, she took a moment to breathe deeply and regroup. She hadn't been prepared for the stab of panic that attacked her when she saw the writhing woman on the bed.

Contractions were a natural part of childbirth. Pain, too. But it still rattled Jasmine to see a woman in so much agony and not knowing the outcome her pain would produce.

A healthy baby, she reminded herself. A big, beautiful, healthy baby to lie in his mother's arms. She couldn't bear even to consider anything else.

"Can you give me a hand?" She gestured to Christopher, who was sitting in a wicker chair that appeared two sizes too small for his long legs.

"She's okay with my being here?" he asked, his voice and his face lined with compassion.

"Sure. And I can use all the help I can get. She's on the verge of having this baby. I've got to check both mom and baby out, then prepare her for delivery."

"You can count on me," he said, tossing his hat onto the chair and moving quickly toward the bedroom. Jasmine followed on his heels, her medical mind clicking into gear, going over the procedures she'd need to accomplish in the next few minutes.

Christopher stepped into the room and combed his fingers through his hair. "You're in good hands, Mrs. Carmichael."

Amanda smiled weakly. But to Jasmine, his words had the same effect as turning on her hair-dryer and dumping it in the tub while taking a bath. She darted him a surprised glance. He'd been told how Jenny died, and she'd bet her last dollar he knew she'd been there when it happened. He nodded solemnly, his gaze full of compassion.

She swallowed hard as he flashed her a reassuring grin. It will be okay, his eyes said. He knew, and he cared.

Amanda grasped her abdomen and groaned.

Jasmine and Christopher broke eye contact and rushed to her side, each taking one of her arms as she breathed through the contraction.

In-two-three-four, out-two-three-four. Jasmine counted the age-old rhythm in her head, verbally cheering Amanda on as the contraction peaked and receded.

"How often are they coming?" Christopher asked quietly, adjusting the pillows for Amanda's comfort.

Jasmine shot him another startled look. *She* was the doctor here. She should be the one asking the medical questions, and he was playacting someone out of a medical drama.

What did he know about a woman in labor? A

tide of animosity washed over her, though she quickly stemmed the flow as she'd been trained to do in medical school.

She knew more than anyone that this was no television show where everything always worked out. The last thing she needed was some couch potato playing EMT.

Christopher's body didn't suggest he spent a lot of time watching television, but his attitude reeked of it. Maybe he just watched medical thrillers.

Amanda smiled weakly. "About every two minutes."

Jasmine settled her attention back on the woman. "Are you more comfortable on your side or on your back? Have you tried walking around?"

"On my side," she said, her voice dull. "I'm too tired to walk." Suddenly she doubled over as another contraction hit.

Christopher looked across the struggling woman and met Jasmine's gaze. "That wasn't two minutes."

"No," Jasmine agreed, "It wasn't. Amanda, I think this baby's ready to meet you face-to-face." Her heart leaped into her throat to do a little dance, then moved up to pound furiously in her skull. This was where the rubber met the road. And she hadn't even assessed Amanda's health yet, or the tiny infant whose life depended on her care.

Jasmine quickly searched through her case for her fetascope and a number of vacuum-packed sterile instruments. She didn't know how much time they had left before the baby would come, and there was a lot to do in the meantime.

"A stack of clean sheets?" Christopher asked, reading her mind.

"Yes, please. And some blankets to wrap the baby in. Warm them in the dryer first. And kick up the thermostat. We need to keep the baby as warm as possible." She wondered again if his baby-birthing information came from the television, maybe an old western. She didn't have time to ponder.

Amanda curled in bed, screaming in exasperation, as another contraction racked her small frame. The hair on the back of Jasmine's neck stood on end. "I hope it's soon," Amanda mumbled through clenched teeth. "I can't stand this much longer."

"You're doing fine," Jasmine soothed, brushing Amanda's sweat-soaked hair away from her forehead. "I'm going to have a listen to this little guy's heartbeat when this contraction is over."

Despite the fact that she hadn't used a fetascope in awhile, she found the baby's heartbeat with ease. It was strong and steady, without a hint of fetal distress. She let out a sigh of relief and offered a silent prayer of thanks.

Christopher returned, his arms laden with sheets and towels. Without a word to Jasmine, he unloaded his burden and began systematically laying out fresh, folded sheets on the bottom edge of the bed, gently moving Amanda's legs when necessary, offering quiet words of encouragement as he worked.

Jasmine took a quick breath and watched him with the woman, amazed by his careful thoughtfulness and the capable assurance of his movements.

He left the room momentarily and returned with several pillows. "I picked up every pillow I could find," he told Jasmine before focusing his attention on Amanda. "These will help support your back while you're delivering," he explained, laying the pillows next to her on the bed.

"Sit up?" Amanda queried with a weak smile. "I don't think I have the strength to move my little finger."

He chuckled. "You don't have to sit up until Jasmine says it's time," he reassured the groaning woman. "Hang in there, Amanda. Breathe through it. You're on the down side of this contraction. You're doing great, and you're going to be a terrific mother."

He looked to Jasmine, a question in his eyes. She answered with an infinitesimal shake of her head.

"Not quite yet," she said, speaking to both of them. "Probably within the hour. But Amanda, this is your first baby. We may be pushing for a long time."

Amanda winced. Christopher wet a washcloth and draped it across her forehead, his soothing tenor reassuring the tired woman.

If Jasmine was honest, it reassured her, as well.

His *presence* reassured her. His instinctive knowl-edge of childbirth was a sight to behold, but that didn't shock her nearly as much as his bedside man-ner. Unlike the proverbial fainting man in the deliv-ery room, Christopher was a pillar of strength, hold-ing Amanda's hand in place of her husband.

"Where *is* Bill, anyway?" she asked aloud in a conversational tone, preparing the iodine solution she would use to disinfect everything and keep the area as sterile as possible. Keeping germs to a min-imum was crucial. She couldn't have another woman die like Jenny had done, and infection was always an issue.

Please, God.

"He..." Amanda paused and gritted her teeth, breathing only when Christopher reminded her "...went out of town for a sales seminar," she fin-ished, gasping as the contraction passed.

She realized too late the kind of question she had asked, how it might affect Christopher. She hadn't even considered the fact that he hadn't been present for the birth of his own son, and wondered how he felt about it now, watching another woman labor. Did he realize what Jenny had gone through to bring his son into the world?

She darted a glance at him. His jaw was clenched, and she could see the anger in his eyes. Anger at Bill for not being there for his wife, or at himself for the same offense?

Jasmine was definitely angry with Bill. What kind

of a man would leave his wife in the middle of no-where when she was due to deliver a baby?

Despite her misgivings, she picked up her thread of dialogue. Even if Amanda was angry at her husband, it would keep her mind off her pain. There was little or no break between contractions now.

Sweat was pouring from Amanda's brow. She appeared as frightened as she was tired. Jasmine knew, from her schooling though not firsthand, that the contractions at this stage were fierce and unyielding.

"His timing could have been better," she said lightly, glancing at Christopher.

At least he had the grace to look ashamed, she thought, noticing how the tendons in his neck tightened as if he were wincing. As well he should be. His own actions were reprehensible.

"It wasn't Bill's fault," Amanda exclaimed, panting for breath. "Not that I care *what* his excuse is at this point!" She stopped and panted. "His boss forced him to go. He'll be so disappointed that he isn't here for the birth."

Amanda cried out. "I've got to push, now, Doctor." Sweat broke out anew on her forehead.

Jasmine checked her again. "You're right, Amanda. You're fully dilated and effaced," she informed her patient, who looked as if she were beyond caring, now that the contraction was over. Amanda's eyelids drooped for the few moments between contractions, and her face was pale and haggard.

It was no wonder they called it labor. Jasmine wondered how a woman could fall asleep between contractions that were obviously wrenchingly painful. Some "experts" said it was a bad idea to let a patient fall asleep, but the poor woman looked so exhausted, Jasmine had to believe that any relief she found must help, be it ever so little.

"Your baby's coming!" Christopher said enthusiastically, gently wiping Amanda's face with a cool rag, and never letting go of her hand. "You'll get to see him any time now!"

Tired as she was, Amanda smiled.

"Christopher's going to prop you up with some pillows," Jasmine explained. "When your next contraction comes, take a deep breath and push for all you're worth."

Christopher gripped Amanda's hands and coached her through several contractions, each one tiring Amanda more. Jasmine wondered how much longer the laboring woman would be able to hold out.

"He's crowning!" she announced excitedly on the next contraction. "Amanda, I see your sweet baby's head!"

Amanda laughed weakly. "Can you...does he...?"

Jasmine smiled. "He's got a full head of thick, dark hair like his daddy," she confirmed.

"Oh!" This time it wasn't so much an expression of pain as it was of wonder.

Jasmine's heart jumped into her throat and lodged

there. A baby was a miracle, and it was a joy to be a participant in the wonder of birth.

But they weren't out of the woods yet, and her mind wouldn't let her forget it, not even for a second. "Let's give another really good push, and I think his head will be out."

Christopher tucked the woman into the crook of his arm and wiped the sweat from her eyes. "This is it, Amanda. Give it your best."

Amanda nodded and gritted her teeth determinedly. "C'mon, kid, let's get this over with," she breathed. "I don't know about you, but I'm getting tired out here."

Jasmine and Christopher shared in her laughter, until another contraction hit and it was time for everyone to go to work. As Jasmine predicted, the head appeared, and she quickly turned the baby a quarter and suctioned the nose and mouth, clearing the air passageway.

"All right," Christopher said calmly, though excitement lined his voice. "The head was the hard part. The rest is easy. Just one more good push, Amanda, and you're finished."

How did he know that? Jasmine wondered again. Christopher continued to amaze her with his medical knowledge.

One more push was all it took. "It's a beautiful baby girl!" Jasmine announced, accompanied by the happy sound of the baby's first wail.

"She's beautiful," Christopher agreed, his voice hoarse.

Their eyes met, and Jasmine was surprised to find he had tears on his face, running unashamedly down his cheeks. Excitement and wonder and joy skirmished for prominence in his gaze. But above all, there was love.

The other emotions confused her. Love made her swallow hard and turn away, focusing her attention on completing the afterbirth and getting Amanda resting comfortably in her bed beside her new daughter.

Again, Christopher was a great help, washing and caring for the baby as if he handled brand-newborns every day. He talked and gurgled to the baby in the helium-high-pitched voice men automatically use with babies. Jasmine tried and failed not to let the scene affect her.

How could she help it? Seeing Christopher holding an infant brought up too many memories. Too many questions. And far too much pain. She gathered her equipment and tried not to think at all.

After spending several more hours monitoring Amanda and her daughter, Jasmine promised to visit her first thing in the morning. Jasmine gave Amanda instructions on what to do if she had any concerns as she prepared to leave.

Christopher interpreted her actions and pulled her aside. "I'm taking you back to the cabin," he said in a tone that brooked no argument.

As if she had enough strength left to argue. She didn't much care *where* he took her, as long as it was warm, and quiet, and she could find someplace to lie down and curl up under a blanket. It was after midnight, and she was physically and emotionally exhausted.

She wondered if Christopher could sense she was near her breaking point. He was solicitous on their way out, taking her bags for her and insisting he keep an arm around her to prevent her from falling on the ice.

She yawned and tucked her head into his shoulder. Tomorrow was soon enough to ask him the questions that had paraded through her mind in constant succession throughout the entire ordeal. For now, all she could think about was sleep.

Chapter Six

Christopher woke to the sound and scent of bacon being cooked in a skillet over an open fire. His neck crimped painfully and his shoulders were unbearably tight from sleeping in the old wooden rocking chair in front of the fire, leaving Jasmine to the privacy of the only bedroom.

He'd carried her in to bed the night before. By the time they'd reached the cabin, she was barely holding on. He'd gripped her hands tightly around his waist for the last mile, hoping she wouldn't slide off the snowmobile. The cold had been her breaking point, and she hadn't made a whimper when he pulled her off the back of the snowmobile and into his arms.

Admiration rose in his chest. She was so strong for others, giving every bit of herself until she was completely drained. She was the type of person who naturally put others' needs before her own. He wished he could voice his respect for her, but she wouldn't believe him anyway.

What saint wanted praise from a sinner? And that's what he was, at least in Jasmine's eyes.

He figured she'd sleep, at least, but it appeared *he* was the slugabed this morning. He yawned and stretched, ruffling his hair with the tips of his fingers.

He couldn't help but enjoy the sight of Jasmine, dressed in the rumpled clothes she'd slept in and looking all the more attractive for it, humming quietly as she turned bacon.

His breath caught in his throat at the domestic scene, the warm, cozy atmosphere she'd unintentionally created. The world had ceased to exist except for the two of them in this cabin. Maybe today, finally, they could work out their problems and move on with their lives. He didn't dare to hope they could move on together. Yet.

"Smells wonderful," he said, moving to crouch beside her under the pretense of warming his hands at the fire. "Breakfast for two?"

He heard her breath catch as she swung her gaze up to meet his. The flash of startled surprise in her eyes stabbed him like a dagger to the chest. The guilty knowledge that he'd placed himself in this position was his penance, his punishment.

He'd have to live with the pain he'd caused her for the rest of his life.

"I was kidding, Jasmine. Relax. I'm not trying to

put you under any pressure." He restrained himself from brushing back the lock of hair that had fallen in her eyes. Her beautiful, shimmering green eyes.

"I know," she said, her voice low. She gave him a wavering smile. "I'm not afraid of you, Christopher."

He swallowed hard, certain his heart had stopped beating altogether. "I'm glad to hear it," he said, his voice gruff.

"I couldn't find any muffins, but I mixed up a batch of pancakes. I thought we could fry some in the bacon grease, if you think your cholesterol can handle it," she teased, a sparkle in her eye.

It was good to see her smile. "You don't have to worry about me," he said, puffing out his chest and flexing his biceps. "I'm the very picture of health."

The smile dropped from her face as she hastily turned back to her cooking.

"What did I say?" he asked gently, laying his hand on her arm.

She shook her head. "Nothing. Can you get the pancake batter from the table?"

"Sure." The message was clear. She wanted him to back off. He was invading her space. He thrust his hands through the spiked tips of his hair and moved to do her bidding.

Grabbing the batter, he handed it to her, then stepped back, folding his arms with his open palms tucked close to his chest. If she wanted room, he had no choice but to give it to her. Even if what he really wanted to do was take her in his arms and erase the distance between them entirely.

"Why didn't you wait for me?"

Her question was spoken in such a soft tone, Christopher wondered if he'd imagined it. But when she turned to him, there was no denying the challenge in her gaze. Challenge, and pain.

He had no doubt of her meaning. She'd bridged the gap between them, said the torturous words that would open dialogue.

And now the ball was squarely in his court. They'd promised to marry as soon as Jasmine's internship was complete. He'd been so young, and so in love, the wait had seemed short. Now, it loomed before him.

"I couldn't wait," he said, surprised at how difficult the words were to say, though he'd rehearsed them a thousand times. His voice was rough and gravelly. "I had no choice."

Her shoulders tensed, and she turned back to her pan, breaking eggs one by one into the skillet. The hiss as each egg dropped into the pan reminded him of the torment of hell he was in.

"Oh, I see," she said finally, sarcasm lacing her voice. It was obvious she didn't see at all.

"Oh, Jasmine," he groaned, slumping back into the rocking chair and holding his head in his hand. The pulse at his temple threatened to burst through, and he pressed against it with the palm of his hand. "If you only knew what really happened!"

She picked up the skillet with a towel wrapped around the handle and slid the eggs onto a platter, then stood and wiped her fingers on her jeans. Christopher dropped his head, unwilling to see her perform such a normal, everyday task when real life was so off-kilter.

He didn't see her approach, but suddenly she was there in front of him, kneeling down before him and reaching for his hands. "I want to know, Christopher. Tell me."

He expected her to yell, to argue with him the way she had the other times they'd met. She had every right to be angry, and she was a spirited woman. But her gentleness, the glimmer of tears in her eyes, was his undoing.

He wrapped his arms around her and pulled her into his chest, burying his face in the glorious silky softness of her thick, black hair.

He inwardly groaned, expressing the agony that was his. For no matter how much he wanted to be with Jasmine, she could never know the whole truth. How could he confess it and risk losing Sammy? It would hurt so many people if the truth came out, including Jasmine. He couldn't be so cruel. He pulled her tighter, closer to his heart.

Jasmine didn't think. She just wrapped her arms around his neck and tangled her fingers in the short ends of his hair. For just one moment, she would give herself the pleasure of being in Christopher's arms again, feeling the strength of his arms like steel bands around her waist, taking joy in the sheer, masculine power of his broad shoulders.

She'd missed him, more than she'd thought possible—until this second.

She'd been only half-conscious when he'd brought her inside his cabin the night before. There was a moment of panic when he tucked her into bed. They'd never been intimate, saving that most precious of relationships for the time when they joined as man and wife; but Christopher was a different man now, and she wasn't sure what he was capable of.

In the end, he'd placed a gentle kiss on her forehead and she'd drifted off into peaceful dreams. If she were honest, it was the best sleep she'd had in months. Sammy was safe with Gram, and though the dear old woman wouldn't get a good night's sleep, Jasmine realized it was probably in everyone's best interests for her to have this night away from all her responsibilities.

She clung to Christopher a moment more, wondering how she could ever have left his side in the first place. If she hadn't gone away to medical school, they'd be happily married right now, probably with two-point-five kids and a dog and a cat.

But she had a dream to follow, responsibilities that went beyond her own limited vision and encompassed the world. At least she thought so at the time. She'd been so sure of herself when she'd expressed these thoughts to Christopher, urging him to go on with his life. It wasn't fair of her to ask him to wait for her.

He'd argued, but she'd been firm, certain she was doing the right thing. Sometimes now she wondered if that vision she'd so readily embraced was nothing more than a specter created by an overzealous teenage girl who desperately wanted to be part of something bigger than herself.

A husband, two-point-five kids and a dog and a cat would never be enough for her. She'd wanted to be a doctor for as long as she could remember, and had never veered from that objective. Again, she questioned her convictions, and came up with nothing but a blank.

Not that it mattered now. She shivered when Christopher moved his head down, his lips grazing the tender skin of her earlobe before planting tiny kisses against the nape of her neck.

With a surprised gasp, she pushed him away. "Christopher, no."

The tortured look on his face was almost enough to send her back into his arms. *Almost* enough. The memory of Jenny's casket being lowered into the ground stopped her cold.

Her stomach lurched, and she wondered if she was going to be ill. Jenny was dead, and she was consorting with the enemy! It was enough to make even the strongest constitution weak and queasy.

Christopher stood suddenly and walked away from her, raking his fingers through his hair. "I'm *sorry,* Jasmine,'' he growled before stomping to the side of the room and slamming his fist into the thick log wall. He winced with the impact. ''What else can I say?''

She remained silent as he shook his grazed knuckles, pressing her lips together to keep herself from murmuring something sarcastic or unkind. She'd never seen him angry enough to punch something. Christopher wasn't prone to emotional outbursts, which made him all the more unpredictable now.

''You can tell me the truth.''

He turned on her, his eyes dark as granite. ''The truth?'' He laughed cynically. ''I don't know what the truth is anymore.''

''No? Let's start at the beginning.'' She paced the room, ticking off a list on her fingers, beginning with her thumb. ''I distinctly remember you saying you loved me, that you'd wait for me as long as it took.''

He grunted in defense.

She shook her head. ''I know. I was the one who insisted we break up while I went to medical school.'' Her throat closed around the words. ''But I didn't exactly mean for you to take up with my sister!''

When he stayed stubbornly silent, she continued. ''I guess any old Enderlin woman is good enough to date, doesn't matter which one,'' she jibed sarcastically.

"I never *dated* your sister!" he snapped back. "Not ever, Jasmine. I was faithful to *you.*"

"Except for when you tied the knot with Jenny, you mean," she corrected acerbically. The knowledge that he'd been intimate with her before their marriage slashed just as deeply as the wedding itself. Maybe more so. It gave a new dimension to her pain, making her feel unattractive and unwanted.

It was irrational, she knew. Christopher had never denied his physical attraction to her, and it was a mutual decision to honor God and wait for the wedding. And she had been the one to break off their relationship before med school. But she still felt he'd turned his back not only on her, but on *God,* when he welcomed Jenny into his arms.

Poor, sweet, innocent Jenny. At least he'd married her when she discovered she was pregnant with his child.

Married her and then abandoned her.

All the old anger came rushing back, and she turned on him, her face flushed with fury and her gaze condemning him before he opened his mouth.

"You said you would listen," he said quietly, shaking his head. "But you've already accused, tried and found me guilty."

"Aren't you?"

He swiped a hand down his face. "I don't know, Jasmine. And that's the honest truth."

"Please tell me you're kidding."

A dry laugh burst from his throat. "I wish I was.

Everything was in such an uproar. But I didn't—''
His words dropped abruptly and he turned away.

Christopher had been about to say *sleep with
Jenny at all*. Not even after the marriage. He was
there to give the unborn child a name and a roof
over his head, and that was as far as it went. Jenny's
health was declining rapidly, to his dismay. But if
everyone knew the marriage hadn't been consum-
mated, others had leverage to use against his claiming Sammy as his son.

"I did things in the wrong order," he said gruffly.
"I'll admit my responsibility to that."

Jasmine winced, then straightened her shoulders
and pierced him with a cold glare. "How gallant of
you."

"I'll tell you what happened," he said, his voice
low and scratchy. "You can figure out the rest."

She nodded miserably and slumped into the rocking chair, wrapping her arms around herself protec-
tively. He wanted *his* arms wrapped around her. But
she needed to hear this story, and she needed to hear
it from him.

"Jenny called me up and asked me to come over
and spend the evening with her and Gram." This
wouldn't be news to Jasmine. She knew how close
he was to her grandmother. "But when I got there,
Jenny was in tears and Gram was nowhere to be
found. Jenny told me later she was out of town visiting relatives."

He was silent a moment, allowing Jasmine to sort

through the issues. It didn't take her long to reach her own conclusions.

"Are you telling me she called you over on a ruse?" she asked, disbelief gleaming from her jade green eyes.

He paced over to the rocking chair and squatted to her eye level, wanting to be sure she could see the truth in his eyes when he spoke. "That's exactly what I'm telling you."

"Hogwash," she snapped. "Why would Jenny need to trick you? She could have just called you."

"Yes. And I would have come. I'd do anything for your family." He'd certainly proved that, even going to the length of ruining his own life in the process. He *had* to win Jasmine back, or his life was *worth* nothing.

He took a deep breath, wondering how to tell her what happened next. "Jazz, your sister was... emotionally unstable. She was a basket case by the time I got to the house. That's the only reason I stayed."

"Jenny was sensitive. She cried easily. But she was *not* a basket case!"

Christopher held up his hands. "I'm sorry. I don't mean to upset you more. I know Jenny was a sweet girl. But she was really upset that night. Smashing glass vases against the wall, turning over furniture—"

He stopped when he heard her sharp intake of breath.

"What…" Jasmine swallowed hard. "What happened? What was wrong?"

"She didn't tell me. At least not then."

She pinned him with a glare.

"I'm serious. She wouldn't tell me. She kept mumbling something about a low-life scumbag, but I never got her to elaborate any further than that. She just burst into tears again."

Jasmine's jaw clenched. He stood and put his hands in his front pockets to keep from touching her. She needed someone to ease the lines of strain from her face, to knead the knots from her shoulders.

Someone. But not him.

"This had something to do with a man?" she asked, her voice choked.

"I believe so. I stayed with her. Cleaned up the mess. Cooked her dinner. She'd calmed down by that time, and…she begged me not to leave her alone."

Compassion and sympathy flashed across her face, replacing the fierce lines of anger. Christopher swallowed hard. Jasmine had the gift of looking beyond the obvious to find the heart of the matter. Hope flared in his chest and his pulse raced.

"So you reached out to her, trying to comfort her, and…" She left the end of her sentence dangling.

"No!" Christopher closed his eyes and willed his emotions to the back of his mind. Her words weren't full of condemnation anymore, but reluctant understanding. "It wasn't like that! You don't understand!"

"I think I do."

"No. I didn't *comfort* her...that way. I went out and rented a couple of those old movies Jenny liked so much and popped some popcorn."

"And?"

He pulled in a breath. "And fell asleep on the couch, somewhere in the middle of the movie. That's all I can tell you."

"A woman doesn't get pregnant by a man sleeping on her couch, Christopher." Her sarcasm was back, a sure sign she was getting defensive again.

Anger tore at him as his face warmed with the necessity of talking about something so personal, so intimate, in such a clinical way. There was no love lost here.

He couldn't tell her why he left, or one of the two main reasons he returned would be null and void. He couldn't let that happen. "That's all I can tell you."

"That's all I want to hear." Jasmine stood suddenly and whisked around the room, gathering her personal items and her doctor's bag. "I'm going back to Amanda's to check on her and the baby."

"I'll take you."

"No," she countered far too quickly. "I want to walk."

"Walk?" he protested. "In case you didn't look

out the window, there's over a foot of new snow on the ground!''

She tilted her chin up and glared at him. "So?"

"So...you can't just go *walking* to Amanda's."

"Watch me."

"Of all the stubborn, mule-headed women..."

She wrapped her parka around her and pulled up the hood. "I'm sure you've known plenty."

The barb met its mark. He clamped his jaw shut and scowled. Stubborn. Mule-headed. And he loved her with every beat of his heart.

"You don't believe me, do you?"

"What's to believe? That Jenny's baby was an immaculate conception? I don't think so, Christopher."

"I'm telling you the truth." He faced her off, his head only inches from her own. Her green eyes were flashing fire. Anger rose in his chest. All their history together, and she couldn't see the truth when it was staring her in the face. Maybe he couldn't say the words aloud, but she should *know*.

The injustice of it branded him through the heart. "You don't believe me?" he asked again. He willed every bit of his heart into his gaze. Surely she would be able to see that of all the people in the world, he could not lie to her. Not now. And not ever.

"As a matter of fact, no," she said, tipping her chin up to pierce him with another glare. "I don't believe a word you say."

"Then believe this." He took her firmly by the

shoulders, tightening his grip when she tried to squirm away. If she didn't know his intentions to begin with, he was aware of the very moment when she read it in his gaze.

He waited until that moment, until she knew what he meant when his lips descended on hers, tormenting him with their sweetness. In his kiss, nothing would be hidden. She would know the truth.

He shifted his weight so he could draw her closer and slid his hands up her shoulders so he could cup her face in his palms, sliding the smooth material of her parka hood away from her head. She was so soft, so sweet, and the unusual, tropical scent that was Jasmine enveloped him.

"And the truth shall set you free." The Scripture flooded his mind even as she melted into his embrace.

Would the truth set them free? In the eternal sense, he knew the answer to that question, but what about the rest of their lives?

She clutched at the front of his shirt like a drowning woman. Instead of pushing him away as he expected, she pulled him closer, hoarsely whispering his name between kisses.

Warmth rushed over him at the sound of his name on her lips. He loved this woman.

He'd always loved her, since the first time he'd looked up into a giant elm and seen her dangling from a branch when he was seven and she was six. Nothing had changed. And everything had changed, leaving him with nothing but the tattered cover of his life. And leaving him without Jasmine.

He broke the kiss off before his passion overrode his good sense, knowing she was too emotionally drained to be the strong one now. He tucked her into his chest and inhaled sharply, trying to slow the runaway rhythm of his heart and steady his ragged breathing. He wanted the moment to go on forever, but knew that his wish went beyond the bounds of reality.

After a moment more, as he expected, Jasmine stiffened and tried to pull away. He caught a glimpse of regret in her eyes and reached for her elbow, but she yanked herself out of his grasp. With a huff of breath, she pulled up her hood and marched determinedly for the front door.

She opened the door and a snowy gust blew in, chilling Christopher instantly. She appeared not to notice, stepping out onto the porch as if it were a bright summer day and not the aftermath of a Colorado blizzard.

At the last moment, she paused, then turned back to him. A single tear slid down her cheek.

His breath caught in his chest as his gaze met hers. He clenched his fists at his sides, hating that he'd hurt her, wondering if kissing her had been the wrong thing to do. He wanted so much for them to be together, but...

"I believe you," she said quietly. "I'm very confused right now. I don't know how to reconcile the facts. But I believe what you told me today is the truth.''

"And the truth shall set you free."

Chapter Seven

"*O*ne more push, Jenny, and you're finished! Your baby is almost here!" Sweat poured from Jasmine's forehead, rivaling that of her laboring sister. Breathing heavily, she wiped the sting of salt from her eyes with the edge of her sleeve, careful not to contaminate her iodine-splashed hands with germs.

"I can't do this anymore," Jenny whispered, her voice cracking in agony. "I can't! I'm too tired to push." Panic in her voice rose to a fevered pitch, then dropped suddenly as her head sagged back onto the sweat-soaked pillow and her eyes drooped closed.

"You can do this," Jasmine said, giving Jenny's leg a reassuring pat. "With the next contraction. Then you can rest all you want." She noticed her voice quavered slightly. She couldn't quite maintain *the clinical detachment necessary for a doctor. Not with her own little sister.*

Well, not so little anymore, she reflected, automatically clearing the baby's airway as she worked. Jenny was having a baby!

Christopher Jordan's baby.

Jasmine felt a slight rush of envy, but didn't allow the feeling to persist. Christopher might be the biological father. But where was he now?

Gone. And it was just as well.

Jenny groaned. Another contraction was coming. One more good push and Jasmine's first niece or nephew would put in an appearance. Excitement mounted.

Jenny rolled up and clenched her jaw as she pushed, but it was not enough to keep her from screaming when the baby slid out into Jasmine's waiting hands.

A perfectly formed little boy. Jasmine counted quickly—ten fingers and ten toes, then cut the cord as the child let out a lusty yell.

Worse than a nightmare, the memory of Jenny's death haunted her waking moments. Jasmine pulled her four-by-four into the driveway of Jenny's house and wiped a hand across her eyes to dispel her thoughts. She sighed and gripped the steering wheel, steadying her labored breath. In the semihypnotic state that driving sometimes induced, she'd let her thoughts run away with her.

Jenny's bungalow was becoming more and more

of a haven to Jasmine, and she was beginning to wonder at the wisdom of selling the quaint old place. She unlocked the door and stepped inside, inhaling the light, lingering scent of cinnamon potpourri— her sister's favorite aroma. Jenny was an almost physical presence here, where her thoughts, hopes and dreams had once meandered through the hallways.

Where Sammy had been born. And where Jenny had died.

Jasmine didn't want to remember the sad things anymore. She was tired of trying to think through the issues, wrestle with the nuances of truth she was learning. She couldn't stop the thoughts from coming, but she continued to shove them into the back of her mind.

That, and trying to forget what Christopher had said. How would she ever sort through the mess that had become her life? His revelation, and her response not only to the words but to the man, had her running from that cabin at top speed, afraid to look back lest her heart become more entangled than it already was.

After visiting Amanda and reassuring herself that the mother and baby were fine, she'd hiked back to her vehicle and made the treacherous trip back into town. She'd spent a couple of hours with Sammy, then she put him down for a nap and headed straight for Jenny's, determined to finish the bittersweet job of preparing the bungalow for sale and get it over with.

Grabbing a box, she opened the drawer to Jenny's nightstand. She'd left this job until last, because she suspected many of her sister's personal items would be in this drawer.

Low-life scumbag. That's what Christopher said Jenny had been mumbling that night. It almost sounded as if she were talking about a man, the sort of statement a woman used in regard to a relationship gone wrong.

But Jenny hadn't been involved in a relationship. Surely not? That she hadn't said a word about a special guy was proof positive that Christopher was lying—wasn't it? She'd certainly never brought a man home to meet the family that Jasmine knew of.

A beat with the echo of a canyon pounded in her temple. She and Jenny were too close for Jenny to keep secrets, especially about romance. Her sister had been the first person Jasmine shared her secrets with, and thought Jenny had done the same.

You kept your engagement to Christopher a secret, her mind taunted. If she'd just told Jenny the truth, maybe none of this would have happened. Jenny wouldn't have run to Christopher, and he wouldn't have—

She cut the thought off. Her whole thread of thought was assuming Christopher was telling the truth. She'd told him she believed him, and she did, though it was completely irrational to do so. Something in his look when he told her the story was so honest, so sincere, that she could do no less than give him the benefit of the doubt.

Of course, his explanation did nothing to the fact that he'd neglected to tell her of his upcoming wedding to Jenny, nor his subsequent abandonment of his wife and unborn son.

With a grunt of protest, she pulled on the drawer, wondering if it would reveal answers to her questions, or if it would merely reveal more secrets to unfold.

It was locked.

"Great," she said aloud, fuming inside. "Calm down and think this through rationally," she demanded of herself, willing her blood pressure to settle. "Where would Jenny put the key?"

She ran her mind over the possibilities. She'd already been through the dresser and the closet. She'd packed Jenny's kitchen items into boxes. She hadn't run across any keys, much less a small drawer key.

She sighed, frustration seething from her lungs. One obstacle after another, with no end in sight. Weariness spread through her bones, dragging her down with its weight. Maybe Gram was right, and she did need a break. But that would leave Westcliffe without a doctor.

Unless...

Jasmine made a dash for her purse and dumped the contents onto the bed. She snatched her date book from the hodgepodge of items and flipped through the pages, then reached for the telephone, which she'd not yet had disconnected.

"Marcus? It's Jasmine," she said without preamble when a man answered. She could tell from the deep sound of his booming bass voice that it was her dear friend from med school, so she didn't see a need to make small talk.

She'd met Marcus White at a campus Bible study during her first year as a resident. When her world had fallen apart, Marcus had been a rock, believing for her what she couldn't believe for herself.

He showed her in the best way, in word and deed, that everything she'd grown up believing wasn't in vain, and that God still worked in people's lives. She wasn't sure she believed it still, but not for his lack of trying.

He knew her present circumstances, at least about Christopher's dumping her for her sister. He didn't yet know about Jenny, never mind Sammy, but that could wait until later. She would explain the particulars when she saw him face-to-face.

She refused to give a thought as to what Christopher might think of Marcus's sudden arrival in her life. She knew he wouldn't be happy about it. Just one more obstacle he had to surmount. At least that's how he'd look at it.

Her eyes clouded as she remembered telling Christopher about Marcus. She and Christopher were secretly engaged at the time, and though he hadn't said anything, the left corner of his lip had turned down. He'd looked for all the world like a little boy who'd just been told to share his favorite toy. She'd kissed him and promised him the world that day, and he'd quickly lost his surly mood.

She shook her head and swallowed hard, dislodging yet another memory. They seemed to plague her today. It was none of Christopher's business who she brought to Westcliffe, she quickly reminded herself. *She* would be happy to see her old friend, and that's what really mattered, wasn't it?

As soon as they'd discussed how Marcus's own plans to return as a doctor to the inner-city neighborhood he'd grown up in had backfired, Jasmine enlisted his professional help.

"I'd be there even if you didn't need me as a doctor," he replied immediately. "I told you that you can always count on me. I'm here for you, girl. You just give me directions from the airport."

Jasmine breathed a sigh of relief. "I'm glad to hear that. I didn't dare to hope when I called you. And of course I prayed that your situation would work out in your home neighborhood."

"I appreciate your prayers," he said, sounding as if he were choking out the words. "Rest assured, God answered them."

Jasmine felt the familiar flare of animosity rise in her chest, the anger that jumped out when she was least prepared for it.

That he was holding back his emotions was blatantly obvious to her, yet his words were filled with strength and calm. For some unexplainable reason, that riled her.

"It was just a figure of speech, Marcus. How can you say God answered your prayers?" she demanded. "You aren't accepted as a doctor in your very own neighborhood. It was your dream."

"That was God's answer," Marcus explained patiently. "He wants me to serve elsewhere. When He's ready, He'll change my dreams."

His voice was firm. He really believed what he said, and that shook Jasmine to the core. She'd once believed herself to have the kind of faith that could move mountains. She made a grunt of disgust.

Deep down, she couldn't deny God existed. The beauty and artistry of His creation was enough to prove otherwise. But she'd come to believe He stood aloof, didn't dirty his hands with the affairs of men and women—at least not common, everyday country girls like she was. Where her life was concerned, she was on her own.

"I wish I had your faith," she said, her tone petulant.

"You don't need my faith," Marcus replied, laughter echoing from the deep recesses of his chest. "You have your own. It just hasn't resurfaced yet." He paused as if giving her time to consider his words.

When she didn't respond, he continued. "Now, getting down to business. What is it you need me to do for you? Tell you to take two aspirin and call me in the morning?''

Jasmine laughed weakly before filling him in. When she hung up, she returned to the locked drawer, deciding it wouldn't hurt to attempt to pick the lock. She tried a hairpin, a credit card slid into the top of the drawer, and the keys from her own chain, but nothing worked. She racked her brain for another idea.

Determined pounding on the front door interrupted her work, and she sighed in frustration. Yet another difficulty was just exactly what she didn't need right now. And she had no doubt it *was* a major trial on the other side of the door. A six-foot, broad-shouldered, sweet-talking problem.

No one but Christopher Jordan and Gram knew she was here. The rigorous beat on the door left no doubt which of the two wanted to see her. And it was not Gram.

"Pizza man," he coaxed from behind the door. "Open up, Jazz, I know you're in there."

"What do you want?" she demanded as she stomped to the door and swung it open. "I'm really not in the mood for company right now."

Christopher tipped his cowboy hat from his head and smiled as he tucked it under his arm, extending the pizza box he held in the other. "Why is it every time you answer the door you bite my head off? Something about knocking make you churlish?

Maybe I should install a doorbell to make things easier for you."

His tone was so light and flippant she had to chuckle, and the aroma of sizzling pepperoni was making her mouth water. "Oh, that would help," she quipped back. "Then you could interrupt me with a bell when I'm loaded under with a ton of boxes, instead of pounding my door off its hinges."

"Man with food doesn't work for you?" His smile was adorably contagious, and she found herself smiling too.

Just food would be best. The *man* in question was already making her heart skip erratically, something she could do without.

"I knew you wouldn't be able to resist pizza," he said, stepping around her and into the bungalow. "I stopped by your place first and talked to Gram."

Sammy! Panic stabbed through her, but quickly ebbed. If he'd seen his son, he sure wouldn't be here now, offering her a pizza.

"She said you hadn't eaten—did you catch lunch in town?"

She sighed. "I haven't been to town. And no, I didn't have lunch. We had a big breakfast, remember?"

He shook his head. "You've got to eat regular meals, Jazz, or you're going to hurt yourself." Placing the pizza box on the table, he tossed his hat onto the counter and pulled out a slice of pizza, waving it invitingly beneath her nose.

"You sound just like Gram," she said, scowling.

Even as she wished everyone would stop trying to run her life, her fickle mouth was watering at the tantalizing aroma. She licked her lips.

"Hungry?" he asked, cocking a grin.

"Starved, actually." She didn't realize just how hungry she was until he'd arrived. She snatched the slice of pizza from him and bit into it, savoring the rich flavor of the mozzarella cheese and the tangy spice of the pepperoni. "Mmm. My favorite."

"I remember." His voice was husky.

She tried to catch a glimpse of his face, but he'd turned back to the table to get himself a slice. "You still haven't said why you're here," she reminded him, a little annoyed and a lot confused.

"Isn't it enough that I want to be with you?"

Her breath caught. "Under the circumstances, I'd have to say *no*."

The smile disappeared from his lips and his eyes turned a smoky gray. "Gram said you might need some help finishing up here."

"Gram talks too much."

"Now, is that any way to talk about your grandmother?" He squinted one eye at her, and she could see laughter lurking just below the surface.

"It is when she butts her nose into someone else's business. Especially mine."

"She's worried about you."

Reaching for a napkin, Jasmine wiped tomato

sauce from the corner of her mouth. "I know she is."

Their eyes met and locked. Christopher's eyes were the smoky blue color that radiated love and passion and made her heartbeat triple. He was a vibrant, passionate man, applying everything he had to whatever he did, just as the Bible said. Whether it be in work, or play—or love. How often had he teasingly reminded her of that verse as his eyes turned smoky?

"In case you're curious, Gram wouldn't let me see my son," he said gruffly, answering the question she hadn't asked.

"I figured."

"I didn't ask." His voice sounded strained, almost tortured, when just a moment ago he'd been laughing.

Her eyes widened. She wouldn't blame him if he'd sweet-talked Gram into seeing Sammy.

When he'd first shown up on her doorstep, her only thought was protecting Sammy from his clutches. But now, despite the myriad of unanswered questions, she wondered at the wisdom of keeping Christopher from his son.

It was clear he cared about the boy, though he'd never seen him. Christopher was acting very much like the man she once knew and loved, the man who put others' needs ahead of his own, who always tried to do the right thing. Who would love and cherish his children.

"I'm not ready," she said aloud. "I know you want to see Sammy, but—"

"He's my son, Jazz."

"I know." *But you ran away.*

The barrier was still there between them, as potent and ominous as the Berlin Wall had once been. She blew out a breath. They'd been down this road before.

She needed more time to think, to sort things out, before she made any decisions. If she allowed herself to be led by her emotions, she wasn't the only one who stood to get hurt. "Did you come here to talk about Sammy?"

He wolfed down another large bite of pizza and shook his head. "No. I came to help. But—" he continued between bites, gesturing toward a pile of boxes "—it looks like you're finished."

"Almost finished," she corrected. "Everything except Jenny's nightstand. I'm going to give it to charity, but I wanted to clean it out first. The stupid drawer is locked, and I can't find the key."

"Have you tried to pick the lock?" he asked, wiping his hands on a napkin.

"Yes, but you're welcome to try again. It's not like I'm a master thief or anything."

"What did you use?"

"Hairpin, credit card, screwdriver. Any other ideas?"

"Do you have any idea where Jenny might have kept the key?"

"I don't have a clue. This is my last project. I've scrubbed this house from floorboards to ceiling, and haven't found a single key."

"Would she have put it somewhere special?"

It was as if a lightbulb had flipped on in her mind, so quickly the answer came to her.

The Bible.

It had lots of pages marked with lumps made by various items—maybe the key was one of them. It was worth a try.

She rushed to the living room, where Jenny's Bible was sitting on top of a small stack of boxes of items Jasmine was keeping.

Jenny's favorite sweater. A photo album to give Sammy when he was older. And she was keeping the Bible, whether or not she ever read it.

She could throw it away, she supposed, but someday, maybe, she would give it to Sammy so he could know a little more about his mother, have something personal of hers, something to remember her by.

His *real* mother.

That he would only remember *her* as his mother both thrilled and terrified Jasmine. And now, if Christopher had his way, the boy would know his father, too. The situation suddenly didn't seem so awfully bad, for the boy, at least.

If Christopher wanted to play a part in Sammy's life, which appeared to be the case, Sammy would be able to benefit from a male role model. But it also meant she would be forced into close proximity with Christopher on a regular basis for the rest of her life.

Any hope she had of getting over him and moving on with her life, perhaps even finding someone else to love, died an instant death in her mind. There could be no other man. It was as if Christopher had been made for her, complementing her strengths and augmenting her weaknesses. She glanced to where he stood, his arms crossed over his broad chest, one shoulder leaning casually against the far wall.

She used to think that he *was* made for her, God's choice for her perfect mate. She squeezed her eyes shut against the tears that burned there, then opened the Bible and shuffled through the pages.

In the middle of it, tied with a small piece of golden embroidery thread, was the key. Jasmine pulled it out and snapped the book closed. "I've found it."

She felt rather than saw Christopher follow her into the bedroom. His gaze on her was almost tangible, and though he remained silent, she knew he felt her tension at the questions yet remaining. She sat on the edge of the bed, her spine stiffly straight, the key poised and waiting in her hand.

It slid easily into the lock, clicking softly as she turned it. "It fits," she said, knowing the verbal confirmation was unnecessary. He dropped his large hand on her shoulder, lightly rubbing the tension from the back of her neck.

The drawer wasn't nearly as full as she expected

it to be. A box of tissues, a couple of paperbacks, a pair of reading glasses. And a picture, an old newspaper clipping that looked like it had been handled frequently.

Curious, Jasmine picked up the photograph. A clean-cut young man dressed in tennis whites with a sweater draped over his shoulder stared dully at the camera, as if annoyed that he was once again being photographed. He was leaning against the railing of his yacht. A smiling bleach blonde had her arms around the man's neck. She, at least, didn't mind being photographed.

There was something disturbingly familiar about that woman, she realized with a start. She looked closer.

"That's *Jenny!*" she said aloud, astonished. Without thinking, she looked to Christopher for help. He merely clenched his jaw and looked away.

How could the woman in this picture be her sister? The Enderlins were a far cry from the country-club type, of which there were none in Westcliffe. A few in Pueblo, maybe, and definitely Denver. But not from around here.

What disturbed her most of all was the foreign look the woman who was her sister had on her face. There wasn't a trace of the sweet girl she'd grown up with. The woman in the picture looked comfortable on a yacht on Pueblo Reservoir where the rich hang out, and in the newspapers. Excited, but not giddy.

Jasmine swallowed hard. "How?" She choked out the word, then gasped for a breath.

"I didn't want to have to tell you." Christopher's voice was low and strangled. Turning toward her, he clenched and unclenched his fists. He opened his mouth to speak, then closed it again, scowling.

She waited, barely remembering to breathe. Her fingers were shaking where she held the worn photograph, the last picture taken of her sister. Nothing was as it seemed. Everything she believed in played her false.

Christopher. God. Now even Jenny. She wondered if she had the strength to hear what he had to say. Christopher reached for her, enfolding her in his arms without a word. Her quivering turned to trembling, and her trembling to quaking as the events of the past few months caught up with her.

She didn't cry. Her tears were spent. But the tension in her body welled up in her like lava in a volcano, finally exploding into tremor after tremor.

He buried his face in her hair and stroked her temple, murmuring until the shock had passed. When she no longer shook, he kissed her forehead and released her.

"Things changed around here after you left for med school," he said, carefully enunciating each word as if the syllables themselves caused him pain. "There are some things about Jenny you need to know."

Chapter Eight

Christopher didn't know how much to tell her. He wasn't sure he should be telling her anything at all. She'd been through so much already. But there was still so much she didn't know.

How could he make her understand how her leaving affected those closest to her? With both their parents dead, Jenny had been dependent on Jasmine, looking up to her as a role model, almost as a mother figure, though they were only four years apart.

All through junior high, Jenny had walked in Jasmine's shadow, doing the things she knew would please her sister rather than developing her own interests. But when Jasmine left for med school, Jenny changed.

Jasmine sat on the bed staring up at him, her wide, green angel eyes shimmering with emotion. Words he never planned to say hurdled over one another to leave his mouth. Without conscious thought, he related the story.

"After you left for med school, Jenny got into trouble. She made new friends—friends apart from the church and the community. She made a lot of trips to Pueblo, staying away for days at a time, even."

"I didn't even know she was hanging out with the jet-setters," she whispered.

"You had all you could do to keep up with your studies," he reminded her gently.

"But I could have *helped* her!"

"Maybe. Maybe not. Jenny had the strong will of an Enderlin, Jazz. She could be nearly as stubborn as you." He tipped up the corner of his lip, trying to smile, but feeling like he was grimacing instead. "I'm sure Gram thought it was just a stage, that she'd grow out of it."

"And she did, didn't she?"

"In a way. When she found out she…was carrying Sammy, she walked the straight and narrow."

What had her sister been seeking? The urge to pull her back into his arms was strong, but he resisted. Since he'd been back, he'd been reaching for her.

This time, he wanted her to reach for him first.

"She went back to church. Got straight with the Lord. Grew up in a hurry so she could raise a baby. She would have been a good mother to Sammy," he concluded softly.

"Do you know the man in the picture?" she queried, handing him the worn newspaper. Steeling himself for what he might see, he glanced at the picture. He had ample reason for his hesitance.

This was the man.

He handed the picture back to Jasmine with such alacrity her eyes widened in surprise.

He'd seen the young man in the photograph, though he couldn't place him right away. He knew it hadn't been with Jenny—he would remember that. The face was familiar, but beyond that he couldn't say.

Bart Pembarton. The biological father of Jenny's baby. That was the man pictured, Christopher realized a minute later.

"I don't think I know him," she said slowly, taking the picture back. She stared down at it another moment, as if trying to read something into the picture that wasn't there. "You know what's odd?"

"Hmm?" he murmured distractedly, his gaze tracing the line of her jaw to her full, wide mouth, which was even now curled down in a girlish frown.

"This doesn't look like Jenny at all, but even so...she looks happy."

"I don't see how."

"Maybe *happy* is the wrong word. Content? No, not that, either. I would have thought she'd be uncomfortable with rich people. But something in her eyes, I guess, makes me think...oh, I don't know. Like she really cared for the man in the picture.

Maybe my overactive imagination is running away with me."

"If you want to believe she was happy, then believe it."

"But you don't."

He clenched his jaw. "I can't say. All I know is that she ran with a bad crowd. She made sure she was quite visible—almost as if she *wanted* you to hear about her behavior."

"I'm surprised I didn't."

"Like I said, Jazz, we all thought it was just a stage she was going through. If I would have guessed—"

"No, you're right," she interrupted. "You had no way of knowing."

Christopher picked up the nightstand and balanced it in his arms. If he stood still a moment longer, he would spontaneously combust. "Where do you want this thing?"

Jasmine pressed her fingers to her temples and squeezed her eyes shut as if staving off a headache. "Out in the living room with the rest of the boxes."

Just before he left the room, he saw her tuck the picture into the front pocket of the flannel shirt she had on over her T-shirt. Anger flooded through him.

He wished Bart were here now. He had two fists to introduce him to. He didn't even want to talk to the man, just show him in a way he could understand what happens when you mess with one of the Enderlin women.

But that was impossible. Bart was dead.

He wanted—no, needed—to help Jasmine. But all he succeeded in doing was to dig himself in deeper. He wasn't able to ease her pain. All he could do was stand by and watch, powerless, as the plot thickened.

More than anything, he hated this feeling of helplessness. He needed to do something, to take some positive action instead of just sitting here twiddling his thumbs.

There must be something he could do. But what?

He ground his teeth in frustration, barely resisting the urge to slam the nightstand to the floor and stomp it to pieces. It wouldn't do him any good to break Jenny's furniture.

Jasmine shuffled from the bedroom, refusing to meet his gaze as he stooped to settle the nightstand next to the boxes.

"Sammy…" she began, then hesitated, looking every direction except at him.

He dropped one knee to the floor, afraid his legs might buckle from the powerful, potent force of the single word. His breath jammed into his lungs and refused to be released.

She cleared her throat and tried again. "Sammy and I will…be walking in the park tomorrow afternoon."

She stopped again, and this time pinned him with a gaze so direct and open it knocked the stubborn breath from his chest in a whoosh of air. "At one o'clock."

Swallowing hard, he forced a trickle of oxygen back into his burning lungs.

Her meaning was unmistakable.

She would let him see the baby!

The memories haunted Jasmine even in her dreams.

Jenny was fading fast.

Instead of the regular joyful recovery of bringing new life into the world, Jenny was growing more peaked by the moment.

Jasmine felt for a pulse. It was weak and erratic. Something was terribly wrong.

"It hurts," Jenny rasped weakly, rolling her head from side to side on the sweat-soaked pillow.

It shouldn't hurt. The baby boy, wrapped in a blanket next to Jenny's side, was wiggling and gurgling contentedly. The afterbirth should have been easy.

Jasmine wiped her hands on a clean towel and stood slowly so as not to alarm Jenny. Her mind was screaming in panic, but her training as a doctor pulled her through. She would remain calm. If Jenny sensed her anxiety, it would only make things worse.

She needed to use the phone, she'd said.

To tell everyone the good news?

Sure. That was it. Her voice quavered with the lie. She'd only be a minute.

But the helicopter couldn't come soon enough. There wasn't anything anyone could do.

Not even a doctor. Jasmine knew it, and so did Jenny.

Her sister had looked up at her with the pained, wise gaze of someone who knew her time was near. She reached for Jasmine's hand, and it was all she could do to keep from shaking, from bursting into tears. From screaming to God for mercy.

"Grieve later," Jenny had said. "There are more important things to do right now." The hospital helicopter was on its way, and there wasn't much time. At least that's what Jenny said. The truth was much harder to hear.

Jasmine merely nodded, unable to speak. She wanted to run, to cry, to scream in rage. Instead, she took her sister's hands and waited.

"I've already made arrangements for my funeral," Jenny whispered, her voice hoarse.

Jasmine felt as if a thousand pins were pricking her body. This couldn't be happening.

Jenny nodded. "Yes. I knew I was dying. I've got cancer, Jasmine."

Jasmine gasped in pain and shock.

"I'm okay with it," Jenny was quick to assure her. "I've made my peace with God."

"How...when?"

"I found out about the cancer the same day I found out I was having Sammy. He's the sole reason I've been hanging on. It's my time, Jasmine. I'm not going to fight it anymore."

"What about your baby?" What Jasmine really

*wanted to say was "What about me?" but she knew
how self-centered that sounded.*

How could she ever live without Jenny?

*Jenny laughed weakly. "He's going to be fine. I
know you'll make the best mother in the world. He's
a lucky little boy."*

*"Me?" She swallowed around the lump in her
throat.*

*"The papers are already drawn up. I want you to
be Sammy's legal guardian." She reached weakly
for Jasmine's hand. "Please."*

*"Of course," she assured, her voice scratchy.
"Of course I will."*

*There was a moment of silence as Jenny's spirit
seemed to fade away. Her breath became shallow
and her eyelids drooped. Then, with what appeared
to be a monumental effort, she opened her eyes and
focused on Jasmine.*

*"Take care my baby." A single tear formed at the
corner of Jenny's eye, then meandered slowly down
her face.*

*Jasmine watched the progress of the salty drop of
water as if in a trance. "You can care for him yourself when you get better."*

"You and I both know that won't happen."

*Jenny's fingers were cold as they squeezed her
hand. "Promise me."*

*"I already did." The sting of tears met with Jas-
mine's stubborn opposition.*

Jenny pulled the infant close to her chest, her

tears coming in earnest now. She stroked his cheek, his nose, his ear, then planted a gentle kiss on his forehead. With a sob, she handed him to Jasmine.

"I'm so sorry." Her words were growing slurred and faint. "Forgive me."

Jasmine wasn't sure if Jenny was speaking to her or not. Her eyes had closed, her face contorted in pain.

"And Jasmine, find...Christopher..."

Jasmine sat bolt upright in her bed, sweat pouring from her brow. Sammy's shrill infant cry had wakened her from the nightmare that was so much more than just a dream. Her breath came in deep, angry waves, her lungs burning with exertion. Jenny's final words echoed in her head, and she wrapped her arms around her legs, hugging her knees to her chest.

And tomorrow—or rather, today, she amended, glancing at the clock on the nightstand—she would introduce Sammy to his father.

She scooped the boy from his bassinet, murmuring gently and rocking him against her breast. She used her index finger to peep through the venetian blinds, which affirmed that the world still lay heavily under the shroud of darkness.

She yawned and rubbed her eyes. Sammy was pretty much sleeping through the night lately. She wondered what woke him, and hoped she hadn't inadvertently yelled in her sleep. She put a bottle of formula in the microwave and settled with Sammy on a rocker, humming softly.

She didn't even recognize the song she was singing, at first, but as the melody progressed, the lyrics soon followed.

"Great is Thy faithfulness…morning by morning new mercies I see."

There was no mercy for one such as she, though seeing the innocent, wide-eyed pleasure of the chubby baby boy in her arms made her wonder.

Where did God's plan end and hers begin? The road was narrow—had she missed it altogether?

She certainly felt she'd wandered off onto some mighty big highway, covered with cars and semis, without a shade of grace or mercy.

She closed her eyes, hesitantly pointing a prayer toward the ceiling, nudging gently to see if the wall between heaven and earth was as firm as she'd once felt it to be.

It budged. No, it did more than budge. The floodgates of heaven opened and God's grace shone upon her like the sun, lighting even the darkest recesses of her heart. The experience was at once so jarring and so gentle that she barely heard the beep of the microwave signaling the baby's bottle was ready.

Sammy heard it, though, and began doing baby jumping jacks in her arms, flailing his round little limbs wildly to get her attention. She opened her eyes and laughed, breathing in the peace that passes understanding. Not really knowing, but *knowing* anyway.

Nothing had changed, yet He had changed everything. She was still meeting Christopher to introduce him to Sammy. They still had a wide gap to bridge between them, and a million details to work out where Sammy was concerned.

What was different was *her*. She'd just made a tiny step toward the right road. A step toward discovering what God wanted her to do. She prayed for the strength and courage to do His will when she knew what it was.

She wasn't the wide-eyed innocent she'd been before she went off to school, she thought, appeasing the squalling baby with his bottle, then settling back down on the rocker.

She was a world-worn woman with a chip the size of Texas on her shoulder. She knew life wasn't full of easy answers. She no longer expected black to be black and white to be white. There were lots of other colors in between black and white.

But then, she reflected, tired but content as she rocked her baby boy, maybe that was why God made rainbows.

Chapter Nine

Christopher was as nervous as a teenager on prom night. After all this time, he was finally going to be able to see Sammy, maybe even hold him. Checking his image in a mirror, he smoothed back his hair with his palm and planted his hat on his head.

He didn't know why he was making such an all-fired effort to look good today. It just seemed right for him to present himself in the best light for his…*son*. The word stuck in his mind and refused to dislodge. He swallowed hard.

It wasn't every day a man met his son for the first time.

He was nervous about holding Sammy, even though his EMT training in Pueblo had taught him how to hold a newborn. He'd been fine with Amanda's baby, but his own son was another question entirely.

Thank goodness Jasmine would be there. She would show him how.

Funny how he fell into his easy dependency on Jasmine after all this time. She was his beacon in the night. Suddenly, he recognized the care he was giving his grooming was as much for her as it was for Sammy.

A family.

No. He wouldn't think about that now. He would meet the baby, and let Jasmine see his dedication to the child with her own eyes. Then she would understand he meant what he said.

The park was a mere five-minute drive from the ranch. He arrived early, thinking he'd find a seat on the bench next to the playground to wait. But when he got there, he changed his mind.

He didn't want to inadvertently put Jasmine on the defensive. Better to wait in his truck until he saw them, so he could approach from a distance, and make sure he didn't catch her off guard.

Not that she'd really be off guard. He knew the herculean effort it had taken her to comply with his wishes. She was offering her trust when no one else would give him the time of day. He wasn't only asking for *her* trust, either, but for her to risk what was dearest to her in the world—Sammy.

His breath caught in his throat when he saw her crossing the lawn toward him. She'd clearly seen his truck, waving in his direction when he looked up. He swallowed hard and waved back.

Her long black hair waved like silk in the breeze, gently caressing the smooth skin of her cheeks. She glanced down at the carriage and made a face, laughing at whatever response she created.

He bolted from the truck, then stopped short at the lilting sound of her croon. "That's a good boy, Sammy. That's my big boy."

He *was* her boy. The knowledge jolted through his system. All of his senses snapped to life, appearing to magnify of their own accord. The scent of fresh-clipped grass assaulted his nostrils, an unusual aroma for the middle of winter in Westcliffe. The wind was crisp and sharp against the edge of his jaw. And Jasmine's sweet voice melted into him like liquid gold.

One thing was sure—she would never give up Sammy. To him or anyone. Without the boy, she would wilt up just as sure as any mother deprived of her infant. He'd already caused enough of a ruckus in the Enderlin family to last a lifetime and beyond.

But he couldn't just turn around and walk away. He wouldn't. He clamped his jaw against a bitter chill that swept through the air. For better or for worse, Sammy was his responsibility. And for better or for worse, Jasmine would have to get used to his presence in her—in *their* lives.

She startled visibly when he tentatively reached for the carriage, her movement as instinctive as a deer caught in headlights. She might be here, but there was obviously still a part of her that was afraid he would grab the baby and make a run for it. That knowledge didn't hurt him as much as the uncertainty in her eyes.

Would he ever be able to prove himself? He resisted the impulse to turn and stalk off the way he came. Frustration and anger seethed through him, vying for prominence, but he held it in check and tipped his hat off his head.

"How is the little nipper?" he asked, awkwardly opening the conversation.

"Good."

Terrific. She wasn't going to help him any. He met her gaze and stepped forward slowly, his movements painfully obvious.

Releasing her breath, she nodded toward the carriage. "I suppose you want to see him."

A low rumble of laughter left his chest as she stated the obvious.

She laughed with him. "That was dumb. Sorry. I'm as jumpy as a rabbit today."

"Me, too," he agreed. Somehow it was easier knowing she experienced some of the same awkwardness he was feeling. Even if it was awkwardness *he* had created.

"You can pick him up."

"I…" He hesitated, unsure of himself. What happened to showing Jasmine what a perfect father he was? He was afraid to pick up the baby.

He scooped Sammy up and cradled his head,

making soothing noises. He tried to remember everything he'd learned. Support the neck. Tuck him in your arms.

Suddenly Sammy pumped his arms and legs wildly, nearly rolling off Christopher's arm. He made an exclamation and grabbed for the boy, who let out a delighted squeal which sounded very much like, "That was fun, let's do it again."

Christopher and Jasmine both laughed with him.

"You don't have to support his neck," Jasmine said. "He's old enough to do that on his own."

"He's a sturdy little guy," he commented, reaching tentatively to touch the baby's hand. His throat tightened as Sammy wrapped his little fist around his index finger and brought it to his mouth, smacking noisily.

"Sure he is. Sammy's my happy baby, aren't you, big boy?" she asked in a sweet croon. "Mommy's big boy."

Mommy.

She called herself Sammy's mother. He supposed he shouldn't be surprised. It was best for Sammy and a natural thing for Jasmine to do, but for some reason it made his throat constrict until he couldn't draw a breath.

"How old is he?" he asked gruffly.

The question made Jasmine scowl. "Three months."

Had it been that long? He would have been back sooner, had he not been in the middle of his EMT training in Pueblo. It had been his way of dealing with Jenny's death, losing himself in his studies, following God's call. But it kept him from Sammy. And Jasmine. Guilt stabbed at his chest.

"Can you show me how to hold him?"

"You said yourself he's sturdy," she replied, the lines creasing her eyebrows together easing as she stroked the boy's downy hair. "Just grab him under his shoulders."

He released the breath he'd been holding and adjusted Sammy, holding him under his arms. Christopher was surprised to discover how heavy the boy was already, and how slippery, when Sammy began wailing and squirming.

He tightened his grip on the boy, still holding him at arm's length. This baby-holding business sure was awkward. "Easy, little fellow," he coaxed.

Jasmine laughed. "He likes to be cuddled close to your body, Christopher. Give your son some loves."

He flashed her a surprised look, but was quickly diverted by his wiggling son. He pulled the boy up to his chest until the baby's soft cheek rested against his rough chin. He gave the boy a hesitant kiss on the top of his head.

To everyone's surprise, Christopher's most of all, Sammy immediately settled down. The baby lounged back into the crook of Christopher's arms and gurgled contentedly, one fist planted firmly in his mouth.

"He likes me," said Christopher, astonished.

"Well, of course he does. Babies know these things, you know. I'm sure he can sense you're his father."

That was stretching it, Christopher knew. He would hate to find out what would happen if Sammy had been exposed to his *real* biological father. Not that Bart wanted anything to do with him.

If only he could tell Jasmine. But everyone was better off if he kept his mouth shut. Sammy was safe, and Jenny's name wouldn't be dragged through the mud.

In all the ways that counted, he was Sammy's father. The baby sensed his sincerity, if not his genetic connection. It would be much harder to convince Jasmine, but he'd manage. He was Sammy's dad, and he'd prove it.

"Does he like to swing?" he asked, gesturing to a swing set.

"He loves to swing," she answered, nodding for him to lead the way.

The three of them spent over an hour playing in the park. He carefully pushed Sammy in the baby swing, laughing out loud when he squealed. Jasmine held the baby on one end of the teeter-totter while he worked the other end. She even convinced him to climb up the ladder and squeeze through a narrow opening to take Sammy down a slide.

He couldn't remember being happier. He was

with his son and the woman they both loved. And they were happy.

He hadn't laughed so much in years, and it was nice to see Jasmine with a grin on her face and a rosy glow on her cheeks. She'd been so unhappy lately.

Somehow the time they shared was unexpectedly intimate, something special only a family unit could experience. He wondered if Jasmine sensed it as well. It was almost as if it were floating in the air, permanently binding them together with every moment they spent together. They were a family.

A *family*. That was the answer.

"I've got to get Sammy back to the apartment. His little hands are like ice cubes."

Jasmine's statement dashed his thoughts and brought him abruptly back to the present. "I wouldn't want him to catch a cold," he said, concern lacing his voice.

She chuckled and adjusted the baby's hood over his head. "He'll be fine, Christopher. I just think we need to be heading home."

"I—" He floundered, having so much to say and not knowing how to begin. "You can't go yet."

She lifted an eyebrow. "Oh? And why is that?" He could still hear laughter in her voice, and he crooked a smile in return.

"I have a question to ask you."

"Ask away, then. I've got to put Sammy back into his stroller anyway."

"Okay." He took a deep breath of the fresh mountain air and hoped desperately the words forming in the back of his throat came out in English and not in some alien language.

Stalling, he crouched down to stroller level and kissed Sammy on the cheek. He was feather soft and smelled so sweet and clean. Christopher had a feeling it was going to be difficult to walk away from the little nipper, even for a day.

"We're off," she said brightly, turning the stroller around.

"Wait!" His heart hammered double time.

She turned toward him, looking mildly annoyed.

"Marry me."

Jasmine's jaw dropped, and she struggled for a good minute to wipe the stunned look from her face. "Excuse me?"

"That didn't come out right," he said, color rising on his face. "I'm sorry, Jasmine. You deserve a marriage proposal with all the trimmings, but under the circumstances, I thought it best to bring up the subject now. Best for Sammy, I mean. And...er...us."

She sat down on the cold grass, not trusting her weak knees to hold her weight. Her insides felt like gelatin. Marry Christopher?

She pulled her knees up to her chest and wrapped her arms tightly around them, as if she might fall apart were she to loosen. She wanted to marry him—it was what she'd always wanted. That was what made the moment so difficult. What she wanted didn't matter.

"Give me one good reason I should marry you," she snapped, deciding to take the offensive.

He crouched down to her level, hat in hand. "I can give you two," he said, his voice low and strong. "Number one, Sammy."

"Sammy?" she repeated dumbly. She didn't know what she expected Christopher to say, but it certainly wasn't to start off discussing his—*their* son.

She shook herself mentally. What else would he be talking about? Surely not love. "What about Sammy?" she asked suspiciously.

"He needs a family."

"He *has* a family. *Me.*"

"I won't dispute that, Jasmine. I've seen today what a good mother you are to Sammy. Great, actually. But doesn't Sammy deserve a home with both a mother and a father present?"

She remained silent, feeling his argument weighing her down like a cement block on her feet. She wanted to bolt from the scene and from Christopher's logic, but instead simply set her jaw and tightened the hold on her legs.

"Don't you see?" he continued, softly pleading. "I can give Sammy a name. I can give him security. I can be a good male role model for him. And most of all, I can point him to his Heavenly Father by being a good father on Earth."

Jasmine shut her eyes, unable and unwilling to meet his persuasive stare.

"I'll do right by him. By both of you. And Jasmine—"

She opened her eyes then, to find Christopher's face only inches from her own. He was looking at her with such love and passion that she couldn't mistake his meaning.

He crooked his adorable grin and Jasmine felt her heart do a loop-de-loop. Why couldn't she resist him? She should, but when he was this close to her, all she could think about was holding him near to her and never letting him go again.

"The second reason our marriage is a good idea is because I love you. I always have, and if you search your heart, I think you'll discover that truth for yourself."

He was speaking the words she wanted to hear. But he was also presumptuously speaking of their marriage as if it were a fact. She embraced the anger that welled in her chest, finding it much easier to deal with that emotion than the frightened tremor of a cornered animal.

There were too many questions, facts Christopher was elusive on or flatly refused to discuss. It was time to throw the ball back at him in spades. "Okay."

"Okay?" He tipped off balance and landed hard on one knee on the frozen ground. "Yee-haw!"

Jasmine cleared her throat. "But before you throw

your hat in the air and start celebrating, you might want to hear the conditions to this agreement.''

He smacked a big kiss on her lips and stood, anxiously shifting from foot to foot. She stood as well, dusting off her backside and cringing at the feel of ice on her jeans. She'd been so steamed up she hadn't realized until this moment how cold the ground was.

She glanced at Sammy, afraid it was getting too cold for the baby, but he was sleeping soundly, his head tilted awkwardly to one side, his breath coming in little white puffs. It calmed her heart just to look at him.

''Honey, I'll do anything for you and Sammy. Just ask.''

''Then tell me the truth. I know why you married Jenny, but why did you abandon her? How do I know you won't do the same thing to me?''

His scowl darkened. He looked like a man frozen in ice.

She nodded. ''I thought not,'' she drawled acerbically. ''What else could I have expected?''

''You could admit your love for me,'' he countered. ''You could follow your heart for a change, instead of rationalizing everything.''

''Oh, like how a man runs out on his wife? That's a tough one to rationalize, Christopher.'' Inside, her heart was breaking, but she was cool and crisp on the outside.

It was happening again, the betrayal, the utter

abandonment she felt when she'd first learned about Christopher and Jenny. The pain felt every bit as fresh and new as it had way back then. Only now she stood to lose Christopher a second time, and with him, Sammy.

Christopher was Sammy's blood relative. His father. She wasn't sure, but was afraid the courts would find in his favor. It was a blessing, really, that he hadn't already filed a law suit. Instead, he'd come up with the ridiculous notion that marrying her would solve everyone's problems.

Well, it would only add to hers. "Then I guess the answer is no," she said, surprised at how even and stable her voice sounded.

Christopher clenched his fists, fighting desperately to control the anger and hurt warring inside him. He couldn't tell her why he left. "Why can't you just love me enough to trust me regardless of the way things look?"

He saw her wince, and reached out to hold her, only to withdraw again when she pierced him with a glare.

"How dare you lay this on my shoulders?" she snarled through gritted teeth.

Because I love you, and I think you love me. He was about to answer when he was interrupted by a man's low bass calling Jasmine by name.

Jasmine whirled around, relief evident in her expression. Christopher broke his gaze away from her, seeking the man that could bring such happiness to her features. He felt his insides crunch as she launched herself into the big African-American man's arms.

"Marcus!" she shouted merrily. "I'm so glad you've come."

Christopher didn't see why she had to be quite so jubilant, unless she was just putting on a show for his benefit. He'd startled her with his sudden proposal, and he knew it. But she didn't have to hang on the man just to make a point.

Marcus kissed her firmly on the mouth, and she joined in his low laughter. He swung her around as if she weighed nothing, then gently placed her back on her feet.

Christopher scowled. Marcus. He'd heard this name before. He searched the recesses of his mind for the occasion.

Of course. Marcus White. Her friend from college. But what was he doing here?

And what was he doing kissing Jasmine?

Chapter Ten

"You arrived just in the nick of time, you knight in shining armor, you," she teased, giving Marcus one more affectionate squeeze before releasing him.

He chuckled, a sound that echoed from the depths of his barrel chest. "You need saving, fair damsel?"

"Call me distressed," she promptly replied.

"And I suppose the man with the stroller glaring daggers at me would be your Christopher?"

"He's not—" she began, but Marcus cut her off with a look.

"Save it for someone who'll believe you."

Jasmine made a face. "I forget how well you know me."

He wrapped an arm around her waist. "Are you going to introduce me, or do I wait until he knocks my block off first?"

They walked arm and arm to where Christopher

was standing, scowling at Marcus and rocking Sammy in his arms.

"Marcus, I'd like you to meet Christopher Jordan," Jasmine said shakily.

"And who's this little fellow?" Marcus reached for Sammy as if he held babies every day, causing Christopher's scowl to darken even more.

Jasmine knew there was going to be an eruption the size of Mount Saint Helens if she didn't avert a disaster here and now. She laid a hand on Christopher's arm and said, "That's our baby, Sammy."

Marcus started so abruptly he almost dropped the baby. "But that's impossible," he muttered under his breath.

Christopher relaxed his posture and reached for the baby. "Nope. This is my son. Say hello to the man, Sammy," he said in a high, tight voice. He waved the baby's pudgy little arm at Marcus.

Jasmine laughed at the astonished look Marcus flashed her. *I'll explain later,* she said with her gaze. He nodded imperceptibly.

"Christopher, I really do need to get Sammy indoors."

He eyed Marcus again, then held the baby to his chest. "I can take him for a couple of hours if you want to—" he stopped and ran his tongue slowly over his bottom lip, eyeing Marcus with distaste "—renew old friendships," he concluded, his voice low and coarse. "I'll drop him at Gram's apartment in a couple of hours."

Jasmine didn't know what to feel, never mind what to say. Christopher obviously loved Sammy, but could he be trusted to care for the boy? What if he ran off and she never found him again? She couldn't bear the thought of losing both of them.

But she couldn't very well confine him, big ox that he was. And even if she could, freedom was a rare commodity. She felt God nudging her to trust Him, and to trust Christopher.

"The stroller converts to a car seat," she said, standing on tiptoe to give Sammy a kiss. When she moved away, Christopher took her elbow and drew her back, brushing a gentle kiss across her lips.

His eyes met hers, and they were gleaming with joy and relief. "Thank you," he whispered for her ears only. "I won't let you—or Sammy—down."

She believed him. Despite his past and the web of mystery still entangling them, she believed him, and her heart was at peace.

"Be sure and buckle him in real tight. Oh—and there's a diaper bag stuffed underneath the seat of the stroller. You should have everything you need—formula, bottles, diapers. You do know how to change a diaper, don't you?" she asked half in teasing and half in distress.

He smiled down at her, his eyes twinkling affectionately. "Think I can handle it."

His mouth straightened to a firm, thin line as he nodded grimly at the other man. "Marcus." He turned away and put Sammy in the stroller, then straightened. "Take good care of my lady."

Jasmine's heart nearly bolted right out of her chest. *His* lady? It gave her shivers just to think about it, but she didn't let herself smile. Instead, she attempted to look every bit as grim as Christopher. "I can take care of myself."

Marcus burst into low laughter. "You got that right, girl."

Christopher just shrugged, indicating his frustration, and stalked off in the other direction, pushing the stroller ahead of him.

Jasmine turned to Marcus. "You, dear friend, are a lifesaver."

"Sweet as candy, you mean?"

She chuckled. "Oh, you!"

"Well, whatever else I am, color me confused. I haven't the slightest idea what just happened over here, but I can tell you one thing—one and one aren't adding up to three, if you know what I mean."

"I told you it's a long story. Things have gotten rather confusing."

After filling him in on the past three months, Jasmine sighed. "I've missed you, Marcus."

He settled an arm on her shoulder. "Missed you, too, girl. I have this peaceful feeling inside me like this is really where God wants me to be."

"I hope so. I need you."

"I'm here in the flesh, girl. Now you just tell ol' Marcus what he can do for you."

"Well…" she begin, then hesitated. "You can't wave a magic wand and wipe the past away, nor can you wipe *my* slate clean, so let's try helping me keep the town clinic running. It's turned out to be more than I can handle with a baby."

"I'm not surprised."

"Yes, well, Gram helps out as much as she can, of course, but she has her own physical limitations to worry about."

"You're living with your Gram?"

"Yes. She was gracious enough to take me in. Nags me incessantly about taking care of myself. She'll be glad to hear you're here to lend me a hand."

"Hand, foot, eyeball. Whatever you need."

"Gross!"

"Sorry. Male humor."

She rolled her eyes. "That's something I don't think I'll ever get used to. Christopher always comes up with the most outrageous—" She cut her words off abruptly, mortified by what she'd said.

Marcus hadn't missed her hesitance, for he squeezed her shoulder lightly. "What are you going to do about him?"

For some reason, Jasmine wanted to break out into bitter laughter. She remained silent as her emotions warred within her, guilt, bitterness, anxiety, anger, pain, grief. She closed her eyes and felt herself weave against Marcus.

He tightened his hold on her. "Question of the day?" he asked seriously.

"I guess." She took a deep breath of the crisp mountain air and let it cleanse her insides. "Christopher—asked me to marry him just before you got here today."

"Really?" Marcus ran his free hand across his jaw. "No wonder he was glaring at me, poor man. What did I do, interrupt the romantic moment?"

"Oh, no, quite the opposite, in fact."

He cocked an eyebrow.

"I was trying to figure out how to gracefully disappear off the planet after I declined his offer."

Marcus dropped his arm from her shoulder and whirled her around to face him. "Girl, you continue to astound me! The guy you moped around med school for asks you to be his wife, and what do you do? Say no."

"It's a little more complicated than that."

"Don't you let a little jealousy get in your way. If Christopher was a big enough deal to mourn about for a year, he's a big enough deal to marry."

"I'm *not* jealous," she denied, even as butterflies of envy fluttered through her stomach.

"Seems like a perfect solution to me. Christopher is Sammy's biological father, and you are his adoptive mother. Christopher loves you, you love him and everyone loves the little tyke. Talk about your fairy-tale endings.''

"Don't I wish.'' Jasmine paused, trying to figure out how to phrase her next statement. "Christopher abandoned Jenny, Marcus. Before the baby was born.''

"*Abandoned* her?'' He brought up a fist and shook it as if threatening an intruder. "Why, I'd like to—''

"We all did. And he was such a good Christian, too.''

"Good Christians don't knock a girl up and then abandon her.''

"This one did.''

"Then why did he come back?''

Jasmine sighed. "I've been asking myself that for days now. Naturally I'd assumed he'd walked away from his faith, but he hasn't, Marcus. I can feel it in my heart.''

"Then what?'' His voice, a deep bass to begin with, dropped another octave, and he scrubbed a hand across the short, tight curls of his hair.

"I don't know. And every time I ask, he clams up like a soldier at Buckingham Palace. All he says is that I need to trust him. Oooh!'' she exclaimed, releasing her pent-up frustration. "I think I'm getting a headache.''

"That's what you get for trying to think,'' he teased, attempting to lighten the mood.

"How would you know?'' she rejoined, glad to

back off from the subject of her life. She'd rather not think about it at all, much less talk about it.

"Do you trust him?" Marcus asked, breaking into her thoughts.

She met his gaze. "I don't know. Right now, my heart is saying one thing and my head is saying another."

"Then wait," he said, grinning to show a full, straight line of shiny white teeth that were enhanced by the dark features of his face. "You'll know when the time is right to act. God will put your heart and your mind in one accord, probably in some incredibly amazing way. All you have to do is wait."

Chapter Eleven

❧

"*What now, Lord?*" Christopher whispered, tucking Sammy's head under his chin. "Where do I go from here?"

He'd spent his two hours with Sammy just rocking him in his arms. His little cabin on the Walters's ranch wasn't exactly secluded, what with all the other ranch hands living in similar quarters all around him. But cozy was just right for the afternoon with his son. He fed him a bottle and even changed a diaper. He'd done well for his first try at diaper duty, even if he did say so himself.

Sure, he put it on backwards the first time, but he quickly realized his mistake and had everything in the right place in no time flat. And no one could accuse him of making the same mistake twice.

He wished Jasmine could have been there to see. Then, perhaps, she would see what a great father he wanted to be. He'd be a great husband, too, but that would be harder to prove. Especially since she'd turned him down flat.

How could he walk away? This baby was as much a part of him as if he *were* the biological father. Sammy was his responsibility. But he was also his son.

Marrying Jasmine had seemed the obvious answer to everything. They could be together, and he could be with Sammy. And it *was* best for Sammy.

Darn the stubborn, mule-headed female race, one woman in particular. Why couldn't she trust him, look past his actions and into his heart?

And to think that this whole blinking mess got started because he was trying to help her sister, thinking that's what Jasmine would want him to do. Remind him never to attempt to read a woman's mind.

So, what was the next step? Somehow, he had to make Jasmine see reason. He had to make her see what a good husband and father he'd be.

Or else he needed to show Jasmine what her life would be like if he and Sammy weren't in it.

He stroked his chin and pondered the thought. It could work. Jolt her so she spoke with her heart and not her head. Whether she was ready to admit it or not, she was meant for him. He, Jasmine and Sammy were meant to be a family. He felt it in the very core of his being.

He tried to focus and pray, but he was too jittery,

unable to sit still. He laid Sammy in the middle of his king-size waterbed, placing pillows on either side of him to keep him from rolling off.

"Sleep well, son," he whispered, kissing Sammy's forehead. "Daddy's home."

He paced the halls for another hour, trying out one scheme in his head and replacing it with the next. By the time the clock struck five, he had a mental wastepaper basket full of shredded ideas.

Glancing at the clock, he felt his shoulders tighten. Jasmine would be expecting him to return Sammy any time now. Well, she'd just have to wait. The boy was sleeping, and Christopher wasn't about to wake him up. He'd wait until the boy woke on his own.

Or at least that was the excuse he gave mentally. Deep down, he was glad he'd be a few minutes late. Maybe missing Sammy would give her time to think. Think about what life without him and the baby would be like. Maybe she'd meet him at the door with open arms and welcome him into her heart and home. And maybe his tennis shoes would sprout wings and fly.

She'd no doubt think he'd up and run off with the kid. His jaw tensed. He'd actually considered it. For at least a millisecond. How could he not, with the possibility of being torn from his son forever lingering on the horizon?

But he wasn't a fool. Running away would be the absolute worst thing he could do. Jasmine already didn't trust him because of the last time he'd left Westcliffe. And the fact that then, as it would be if he left now, there had not been a single moment where his soul didn't long for Westcliffe and to return to Jasmine's side, wouldn't hold much weight with her.

If he ran, it would be with the thought of eventually reconciling with Jasmine. But if he ran, reconciliation could never happen. So he had to find another way.

There *was* another way. It came to him clearly and quietly, a way to startle Jasmine into searching her heart for the truth. She'd mentioned it herself the first night he was back.

It was difficult to consider the option, but what other choice did he have? He had to do something to shock her. And this was going to make Jasmine fighting mad.

"Where is he?" Jasmine demanded for the tenth time in as many minutes. She peered through the front window shade, watching the parking lot below for lights or movement.

Marcus was stretched out on Gram's sofa, snoring quietly. Gram was sitting in a rocking chair, sipping at a cup of hot tea.

"You're sure you knew what you were doing when you let him take Sammy?" Gram asked, her voice scratchy. She often coughed at night.

"Of course I knew what I was doing!" she

snapped, then grimaced. "Or at least I thought I did. What's taking him so long? Do you suppose they got in an accident?"

"He's probably just enjoying time with his son, Jasmine," Gram said gently. "It's their first time alone with each other. Don't rush them. Besides, you should be enjoying this time off baby duty. It's going to be nice to have another parent around."

"He sure swung you over to his side in a hurry," she commented acerbically.

"I wasn't aware there were sides," Gram snapped back, every bit as brittle.

Jasmine sighed. Even she had to admit the sides were getting a little gray around the edges.

"Why don't you grab a cup of tea and sit down? We haven't had a good chat in ages."

Jasmine did as she said, feeling more relaxed just holding her steaming cup of tea.

"That Marcus fellow is certainly nice," Gram said in a transparent attempt to change the subject.

"Yes. He's a good friend. It was really great of him to agree to help me out at the clinic. I hope you don't mind his crashing here overnight until he can find a place to live."

"I'm always open to entertaining strangers," Gram agreed quickly. "You never know when you're going to offer your hospitality to an angel."

Jasmine laughed. "Marcus is a real sweetheart, but he's hardly an angel. He'd be the first one to tell you that. But I'll concede he's prayed me out of more than one pinch. His faith in God is strong."

"Is that the only reason you invited him?"

Jasmine stiffened. "If you mean do I have feelings for Marcus, no. At least, not in that way. We are dear friends, and that's all we will ever be. He knows how I feel about—" She wasn't about to finish *that* loaded statement.

"Christopher," Gram concluded for her.

She winced, folding her hands in her lap to keep them from shaking. Gram would notice her anxiety in a moment if she wasn't careful to hide it from her.

"But that wasn't what I was asking. It appears to me you might use Marcus to hide behind so you don't have to deal with said *problem*."

Jasmine didn't fail to notice how Gram avoided speaking Christopher's name a second time. "I'd never do that to Marcus!"

"Maybe not intentionally, honey, but it would be easy to do without even meaning to."

"I don't think so."

"Think about it. You and Marcus are close. It would be easy to give Christopher the opinion you were more than friends, without ever letting on to Marcus what you were doing."

"What are you getting at, Gram? Are you trying to plot me a way to get rid of Christopher for good?"

"No, of course not. I'm just trying to point out

what might happen. You're bound to get hurt. You could lose Christopher *and* Marcus.''

''I don't *have* Christopher,'' she denied, her mind freezing on the first part of Gram's statement.

Gram cocked a silver eyebrow. ''No? I've got news for you, sweetheart. That man loves you within an inch of his life.''

''I don't see what difference that makes.'' Gram of all people knew how impossible the situation was.

''It's your call, Jasmine. I just want you to remember the Lord's admonition to forgive. Christopher has done a lot of bad things. But he's back now, and it looks to me like he's trying to atone for his sins.''

''I don't know what that means to me.''

''Give yourself time. God will help you work it out.''

She had God to help her work it out. That was a comfort, anyway. She'd been praying and reading the Scriptures every day since she'd made a commitment to walk in His steps. He'd been opening her heart to considering new paths.

It was part of the reason her feelings about Christopher were so contrary. And another of the many reasons she could not even consider marrying Christopher at this point.

''I've been feeling restless lately,'' she admitted quietly.

Gram nodded.

''I always thought the only thing I wanted in the

world was to become a doctor and move back to Westcliffe. I wanted to be a country doctor, taking care of the people I've known all their lives. I wanted to bring all my high school friends' babies into the world. I've never even considered any other path. But lately..."

"You've discovered there's more to life than just your career."

"Yes, for starters. I'm sure you remember how much a newborn baby changes your world. I view everything as a mother now, not just a woman. Family means more to me than I expected."

"Enough to give up your career?"

"No. I don't think I could ever give up being a doctor, at least in some capacity."

"Dr. Mom," Gram teased.

"I don't think that's quite enough," she said, laughing. Tears followed close behind the laughter, for no reason she could fathom. "I'm a small-town girl who is strongly tied to her roots. I love the Wet Mountain Valley, the beautiful mountain range. History runs through the town like Main Street itself. Two years ago, I was pining for home, thinking that once I was back I would never want to leave Westcliffe again."

"Come here, love," Gram whispered, opening her arms.

Feeling like a young, frightened girl again, Jasmine knelt before her grandmother and laid her head against the old woman's breast. She closed her eyes, inhaling the powdery scent that was distinctly Gram, and losing herself in the gentle caress of Gram's hand on her hair.

"I think God's calling me somewhere else," she admitted, reaching for a tissue.

"Any place in particular?"

She wiped her tears away, her mind wandering to the missionary information packets she'd been studying in every bit of her spare time. "I think I'm going to take Sammy and go to Ecuador."

She expected Gram to be surprised, but she just nodded like a sage old owl.

"Why do I get the feeling you already knew this?"

"I didn't know where. I just knew. Why Ecuador? Are you going down as a doctor?"

"There's a hospital in Quito. And I already know Spanish. I learned it in college and used it a lot in Denver at the hospital."

"I'm glad you're seeking God again, Jasmine."

She smiled through her tears. "Me, too. But I'm scared to death to be stepping out in faith."

"He's ahead of you, on the left and right of you, and behind you as well. He's your fortress, and a twenty-four-hour-a-day watch guard. Rest in Him."

"I will, Gram." She blew out a breath. "Whew. It sure is nice to have that off my chest. I do worry about you being here all alone."

"I'm not alone. God is here. And I have lots of friends in this town. I was born here, you know."

And I'll die here. The words were left unsaid, but hovered in the air anyway, putting a damper on Jasmine's rising mood. She made a mental note to explain Gram's situation to Marcus when she talked to him, so he would look in on her regularly.

That is, when she had that big, long, unavoidable heart-to-heart talk with Marcus. The mere thought of it made her stomach cramp. What would he say when he learned she was prepping him to replace her rather than just help her out?

Her thoughts were interrupted by the doorbell. She jumped to her feet and lit to the door like someone had set her tail on fire. Behind her, she was aware that Gram had stopped rocking, and that Marcus was wearily rousing himself on the couch.

No one said a word, but she knew they'd all thought the same thing. Deep down under layers of reassurance was the lingering doubt that Christopher might have been planning to steal Sammy away all along, and she had conveniently handed the baby right into his hands.

"Christopher," she announced loudly as she swung open the door, her hands shaking with relief. Her heart wanted to burst with happiness when she saw him and the baby, but instead, she scowled. "You're late."

"Sorry, Mom," he replied, tipping his hat back and giving her that toe-curling grin of his. Her heart was hopeless to resist his physical presence, but her mind was pressing for answers.

"This is where you come into the house, remove Sammy from his seat and give me a really good excuse why you thought it was okay to worry me half to death."

"I had you worried?"

"A figure of speech, I assure you."

Gram burst into laughter, but when they both turned to her, she was looking away out the window and humming softly to herself.

"The little nipper was sleeping," he offered, unbuckling the straps on the baby carrier and lifting Sammy out of the seat. He kissed the baby's cheek and handed him to Jasmine.

Her heart immediately settled now that Sammy was back in her arms. He was a perfect fit. His sweet, baby scent was pleasant to her nose, and his happy squeal music to her ears. She really was becoming a mother.

She didn't feel quite whole without him any more. And maybe just a little of it had to do with Christopher being here with her as well.

"Were you giving your daddy a hard time?" she asked Sammy, who bounced and kicked in her arms.

"Da!" he said, then, pleased with himself, said it again. "Da!"

Christopher whooped in delight. "Did you hear that? My baby boy just called me Dad!" He thrust his chest out like a rooster and strutted around the room. "How 'bout that? Sammy's first word is *Daddy*."

He couldn't have been grinning any wider, Jasmine thought, somehow irritated, feeling as if she'd been betrayed. Of course the baby didn't know what he was saying, and she'd be hearing *Mommy, Mommy* soon enough. Still...

He pulled his hat off his head and rolled the brim in his fists. "Will you walk me out to the porch?" He glanced covertly at Gram and Marcus.

She stared at him wide-eyed for a moment, then nodded slowly. "As long as you promise this won't be a repeat of this afternoon. I can't handle that yet."

"Oh, it's definitely not a repeat of this afternoon," he muttered under his breath.

"In that case, let me give Sammy to Gram and I'll be right there."

He nodded and planted his hat on his head, sauntering out to the porch. He took deep breaths to try to slow his heartbeat. It was downright cold once the sun went down. He could see his own breath coming in white puffs of mist, and the breeze nipped the skin on his face despite his five o'clock shadow.

She appeared suddenly, and immediately wrapped her arms around herself against the cold. Christopher wished he'd thought to remind her to bring a coat out with her.

"I won't be long," he promised.

"Um, okay," she said, looking perplexed. Her bottom jaw was starting to shiver. She looked small, defenseless and entirely adorable.

He put his hands on her shoulders and rubbed down her arms to help restore the circulation. Then he lightly swept his fingers back up her shoulders and cupped her face in his hands. He brushed a light kiss on her forehead, her nose, her lips, her jaw.

Then he took a deep breath and plunged ahead. "I can't live without my son, Jazz," he began.

"I don't expect you to."

"But you won't marry me."

She stiffened in his embrace. "You promised you wouldn't ask me that. I can't think about it right now."

"I wasn't asking, just stating facts. I know you feel it's more than you can handle right now, but it really is the best thing for everyone concerned."

"I asked you not to talk about it anymore," she snapped, turning away and staring off toward the shadowy, jagged outline of the Sangres.

He moved up behind her, putting an arm around the front of her shoulders and drawing her firmly against his chest.

She stiffened in his arms, but didn't try to move away.

"Can you really not trust me?" he asked, his voice husky. "Isn't it enough that I've returned?"

"No. And no. You've given me no reason to trust you, and how am I supposed to know whether or not you are staying for good?"

He *wouldn't* be staying in Westcliffe for good. It

was part of what held him up from returning for Jasmine and Sammy. But now wasn't the time.

"What if I told you leaving was something I had to do, that it wasn't meant to hurt anyone? And that the reasons are, at this point, beyond explanation?"

"In other words, you plain just don't want to tell me. You don't trust me, but you want me to trust you. To be your wife." She turned in his arms until they were face-to-face. She looked up at him, confusion rampant in her deep green eyes.

He wanted to forget his intentions and kiss Jasmine like he did in the old days, when they dated in high school.

But he was a man now, and the kiss he would give her would be a man's kiss. It was far too dangerous to risk. His self-control was thread thin as it was. And he had an agenda tonight.

Cupping her hips, he pushed her back a step. She stroked a hand down his face and sighed. "Don't you see, Christopher? I can't marry you with secrets between us. A husband and wife are one. They should share their lives in every way, and that includes trusting the other enough to tell the truth."

Her voice cracked and she stopped, nibbling on her full bottom lip as she considered what to say next. "If you believe I love you, then you've got to know that whatever dark things are in your past, I can hear them. I can forgive you. And I'll go on loving you."

It was incredibly tempting just to blurt out the

truth and have it done with. He more than anyone was sick to death of keeping secrets. If it would be like Jasmine said, he'd willingly divulge the whole agonizing truth.

If she loved him and forgiveness was real, she'd understand why he'd kept silent, and would join in his silence to keep Jenny's memory untarnished and Sammy's reputation pure. There would be no more bitterness between them. They'd marry and raise a big family, with Sammy as their eldest son.

But it wouldn't happen that way. Anger would overwhelm the lesser sentiments, and then Jasmine wouldn't allow him to see Sammy at all. If he told the whole truth, she'd have ample authority for making it so Christopher never saw Sammy again.

And that, he could not risk. It wouldn't be right. He owed it to Sammy to keep the truth to himself. More important, he loved the boy.

"I can't tell you, Jazz. I'm sorry, but I can't."

"Then it appears this conversation is over. I'm freezing out here, anyway. Good night, Christopher." She ducked under his arm and started toward the door.

"Wait!" he called, reaching for her elbow to stop her. "If you won't accept my marriage proposal, what are we going to do about Sammy?"

"Sammy?" she asked, looking perplexed. "Oh, I see. You mean can you see him again?"

Christopher nodded.

"You've proven yourself, as far as I'm concerned. We'll make plans for you to see him on a regular basis. Every other weekend or something.''

His jaw dropped, then he clamped it shut. He was good enough to see Sammy every other weekend? What was this, some kind of contest or something, and Sammy was the door prize?

''Why don't you go out and buy yourself some baby furniture? You can use my car seat-stroller, but you'll need a crib, some baby blankets, diapers and a few toys.''

She sounded so detached, too clinical. He yanked his hat off and slapped it angrily against his thigh. ''I'm afraid every other weekend isn't good enough for me.''

''What's that supposed to mean?'' she snapped, sounding alarmed.

''It means if you won't marry me, I'm taking you to court for full custody of Sammy.''

Chapter Twelve

The cabin was cold and empty when Christopher returned. He poked at the ashes inside the wood stove in the corner and got some kindling ignited, then slumped into his large easy chair and spent ten minutes staring blankly at the television and channel surfing with no real heart.

He was bluffing, and he was more afraid than he'd ever been in his life.

The whole thing was nothing but a ruse to catch Jasmine off guard. It had as much chance of failure as success—the act of a desperate man.

He looked around at the cabin and snorted in disgust. This place wasn't fit for anyone, much less a tiny baby. Besides, it wasn't his. He couldn't even imagine what the Walters would have to say about it if he brought a baby on their land.

He supposed he could look for something else,

except he really wasn't looking for something more permanent. Because he wasn't going to be staying in Westcliffe.

Now, however, it looked as if he *would* be staying, at least until he could prove to Jasmine his heart hadn't changed, that he wasn't the scoundrel of a man who walked out on her sister. He was still the man she had once loved and to whom she'd pledged herself.

He wasn't leaving without Jasmine. And if that meant another six months or another six years, then so be it. God's timing was better than his, he knew, but he was impatient.

He'd played his ace. Now all he could do was sit back and see if he won the hand. This was Dead Man's Draw, winner take all.

The irony of it was the secret he was carrying was the reason he *couldn't* take Jasmine to court for custody of Sammy. There, under oath, he would have to tell the world that he was not Sammy's father. And even if he lied, which he wouldn't do under oath, the paternity test they'd no doubt make him take would be just as revealing, probably more so.

And in Westcliffe, real news was scarce. They were sure to make the front page of the newspaper, maybe even as far as Pueblo. And Sammy would become a public entity.

He couldn't let that happen. He *wouldn't* let that happen. Bart Pembarton hadn't been man enough to own up to what he'd done, to do the right thing, marry Jenny and claim his son—not when Mommy and Daddy might object. And object they did, when Christopher confronted them with the facts after Bart's death. Bart's parents had warned Christopher not to let Sammy become a public entity. He sensed their threats were real. No matter what, Christopher had to protect Sammy.

Without realizing where his thoughts were heading, the night of Bart's death replayed in his mind, as clearly as if it had happened yesterday. It was a hot, damp night in Pueblo, and he'd been working on duty as part of his EMT training.

They'd been called to the scene of a fatal traffic accident. The wreckage was a once shiny BMW lodged between a light pole and a building, as if the driver had been attempting to drive on the sidewalk.

There were no drugs or alcohol involved, and the fatal accident remained shrouded in mystery. But the driver had been the man in Jenny's photo. Why had Bart crashed his car?

Christopher's stomach knotted. He'd made a decision to forgive the man for getting Jenny pregnant. It was a conscious struggle to make that decision truth. He still got angry just thinking about it. But forgiveness, he reminded himself, was an act of the will. His feelings would eventually fade, and God would help him through.

Responsibility definitely hadn't been Bart's middle name. Of course he hadn't wanted a child to slow down his jet-set life-style, especially with his parents holding the purse strings.

The Pembartons might have money, but money wasn't what a child needed most in life. Only he and Jasmine could give Sammy the home he deserved. He knew he couldn't do it alone. The picture wasn't complete until Jasmine was in it, binding their hearts together as one.

Which is why he'd taken so great a risk in announcing he was taking her to court. The last thing he wanted to do was hurt her, and he knew his words had hurt her. But it couldn't be helped. He'd tried affection, now he hoped intimidation would work.

If it didn't, he was in a world of trouble. He clenched and unclenched his fists, wanting to punch something just because it was there.

He was a man of action, and he'd just relegated himself to sitting back and waiting for Jasmine to come to him. All he could do was pray she'd want to talk about a compromise, which would give him another chance to convince her marrying him was the best solution.

If only he didn't hate waiting so much.

"Oooh! That lousy, no-good, rotten—" Jasmine vented, stomping across the floor and back again. "If he thinks he can intimidate me, he has another think coming."

Marcus grinned up at her from the kitchen table, where he was eating a big bowl of oatmeal. "You were so quiet last night, I knew there was something wrong.''

''I didn't want Gram to worry. But Marcus, what he did to me last night was like a slap in the face.''

He chuckled, a low, deep sound from his chest. ''You haven't exactly let the cat out of the bag yet, girl. What exactly did he do?''

''He said he's suing for full custody of Sammy.''

''He wants *full* custody? He wants to take Sammy away from you?'' he said quietly, in wonder. Then he took her firmly by the shoulders and reassured her with the strength of his gaze. ''You've got rights, Jasmine. And friends who will fight tooth and nail to keep Sammy with you. Myself being first and foremost, of course.''

''I know.'' She sighed wearily. It had been a long, sleepless night, fighting emotions that ranged from passionate, self-righteous ire to fear and apprehension such as she'd seldom known before.

She'd spent at least an hour raging in her own fury before it occurred to her the best thing to do was to seek a Higher Authority in the matter.

She'd sought God on her knees, begging for His interference in her cause. She knew that God, more than anyone on this earth, understood what it meant to be separated from His Son.

She'd pondered through the middle of the night on the incredible mercy and love of a God who would give His own Son to die in her place. What sacrifice Jesus made for her, to come down from heaven and be made a Man. And His Father willed Him to go.

She knew she was not that strong. She couldn't give Sammy up, not even to Christopher, who she knew would love and care for the baby.

She prayed for peace, and she prayed for answers. But by morning she'd still not been able to come up with any long-term solutions to the problem, short of running away and changing her name as she'd seen ladies on television crime shows do.

Would she be a hunted woman? Would Christopher put the FBI on her case? Her mind had raced with the possibilities, and the questions answered themselves.

She couldn't force Sammy to live that way, living hand to mouth and always looking behind her for shadows. It wouldn't be fair to him. She had to find another way to fight Christopher and keep Sammy.

"Are you taking me to the clinic today?" Marcus asked, cutting off her thoughts.

"Actually, today would be perfect. I'll show you around and get you settled. This afternoon I've really got to try to hook up with one of those charity organizations in Pueblo so they can come by Jenny's bungalow and pick up all her things."

Marcus nodded, but didn't comment.

"I hate to be leaving you on your own on your first day, but the county nurse will be there, and being such a small town, the receptionist is very knowledgeable."

"No problem. Relax."

"Of course, I'll be wearing my pager, and I always have my cell phone with me, if you have a problem."

He barreled out a deep, hearty laugh. "Will you *relax?* I've been alone in a clinic before. I think I can handle it. Besides, I'm getting kinda fond of this country living."

"You've only been here a day."

"Fondness grows quickly. I feel like I'm home here in Westcliffe, with its horses and hayfields. Funny for a man born and raised in the ghetto, I guess. But I can't help it. This place just feels right to me. Like I could put down roots here. It'd be a great place to raise children," he concluded, with a pointed look at Jasmine and a sly grin.

She was relieved to hear it, more than he could possibly know. That Marcus might want to stay on as the doctor for this town was looking like more and more of a possibility.

And if that happened, she'd have the freedom she desired to pursue the new dreams God had given her. If she could work things out with Christopher and Sammy. At the moment she was bound hand and foot.

She had three choices. She could run, but she'd already ruled that one out. She could go to court, but with Christopher's paternity proven, she had the sinking feeling he'd get Sammy in a heartbeat, no matter what she said on the witness stand.

The other option, and the one that galled her to the core of her being, was that she could go back to Christopher and beg. Beg for time with Sammy, even if it were just every other weekend, as she had suggested Christopher do.

For a moment, she found herself in his shoes, only able to see their son once every two weeks, and then for only a couple of days at a time. It was no wonder he'd said it wasn't good enough. If he felt even half the agony that she did at the thought, his heart was being ripped out of his chest in little pieces.

It startled her to have put herself so much in Christopher's position, and she immediately shut down her thoughts and emotions on the subject. Her only desire and responsibility was to see she kept Sammy, whatever the cost.

"You look like that famous thinker statue guy. The de-e-e-ep thinker," he said in an exaggerated tone. "Keep that up and you're going to make your headache worse."

"Are you ready to go down to the clinic?" she asked, her voice sounding annoyed despite her best efforts.

"Not thinking about Christopher won't make him go away," Marcus said gently. "Eventually you are going to have to face him again and try to work this out."

"That may be," she snapped, seething in frustration. "But I don't have to think about him, talk about him or most especially talk *to* him, today. I would appreciate it if you didn't bring his name up again."

"Hey, girl, whatever you say," he replied easily, ignoring her tone. "I think we ought to get to the clinic right away. Do you think I might be able to search out a place to live after work?"

"Well, sure. The clinic closes at three today."

"I'm looking to buy, Jasmine. I hope that doesn't alarm you."

"On the contrary, I'm very pleased."

He opened the front door and gestured her through. "After you, Dr. Enderlin." She'd been called a doctor since the beginning of her internship, but suddenly the title felt too tight, as if it were strangling her.

Funny how something she had worked so hard for and been so single-minded about could feel so awkward and uncomfortable to her now.

Well, no matter. She loved being a doctor. At least *that* hadn't changed. She'd just discovered there was a big, scary world out there and shades of gray all over the place.

"Jasmine? Are you coming?" Marcus asked in his soft, low voice.

Jasmine. At this point it was all she could do just to be Jasmine, never mind mother, doctor, friend. And now Christopher was asking her to be his wife. She wanted to scream in frustration.

That is, if he still wanted her as his wife. Taking her to court was a pretty drastic move in the opposite direction. But she wouldn't think about that now, she reminded herself again.

Today, she would just be Jasmine. Okay, and Dr. Enderlin, at least for the afternoon.

As it turned out, Jasmine wasn't able to contact a charity group in Pueblo as she'd planned. An avalanche at the nearby ski resort kept Marcus and her busy well into the night, tending to major wounds, X-raying broken appendages and arranging for helicopter flights and ambulances for those who needed to be hospitalized.

Days flew by as Jasmine made rounds, introducing Marcus and caring for the less serious injuries. It seemed to Jasmine that at least a third of the town had been skiing that day, though she was certain she was overestimating.

Her real surprise was in Marcus. She already knew he was a fine doctor with a heart for the people, but she was truly amazed at how well everyone had taken to him. She'd heard compliment after compliment from those healed by his medical expertise.

He was so patient with the children, kind to the elderly and straightforward when a patient needed to hear something about their recovery. More than once she'd just hovered in the background and watched him work his magic on others.

Marcus found a house, and because it was vacant,

the closing went quickly. At the end of the first week, he'd moved into his new home.

By the end of the second week, Jasmine was physically and mentally exhausted. The only good thing was that she hadn't had time to think about Christopher. She checked on baby Sammy during her lunch hour and tried to spend time with him in the evening, but more often than not she fell asleep on the rocking chair with a wiggling, bouncing Sammy in her arms.

Marcus insisted that she take a week off. The clinic had slowed down to a dull roar, and she needed time to recuperate so she could be at her best for Sammy.

She didn't even argue, which was very unlike her. Instead, she went to bed and slept for two days, rising only to eat and care for Sammy. Gram assured her everything was under control and that Jasmine should rest before she became ill.

It wasn't until after her extended session of sleep that she felt ready to face the world again, and the first order of business was finding a charity to take care of Jenny's things. After arranging for one to come that afternoon, she put a sandwich together and took off for Jenny's bungalow.

As always, the smell was the first thing that caught her when she entered the house. Jenny's smell. She wondered why a house would have the owner's smell about it once the owner was gone.

She didn't notice any smell in her own house. She wondered if others did, and if so, what kind of smell hers was.

Jenny's was light and breezy, just as Jasmine remembered her personality as being. But then she remembered the newspaper photograph.

The newspaper photograph! What had she done with it? Her hand flew instinctively to her left breast pocket, where she vaguely remembered placing it. But of course it wasn't there now, since she wasn't wearing the same clothes.

What *had* she been wearing? She strained to remember. She'd worn her grubbies that day, which meant...

The jeans with the holes in the knees. A black T-shirt. And...

Her red plaid flannel shirt. That was it. The photograph was in the pocket of her red plaid flannel shirt. Except, where *was* her flannel shirt?

She leaned against a wall and slid slowly to the floor, cupping her face in her hands. How could she have been so stupid as to lose the picture?

She was overreacting, she knew. It was just a lousy newspaper photograph, and not even one that showed Jenny in her best light. But for some reason, it was important to Jasmine, a part of Jenny that she wanted to keep.

Odd as it seemed, she felt it must have meant something special to her sister, being locked up in her nightstand as it was. She could just picture Jenny carefully unlocking the drawer and pulling out the picture, staring at it with the glassy-eyed look of someone in love, and then hugging it close to her heart with a sigh.

She threw her head back until it was touching the wall, and it was there that she spotted her red plaid flannel shirt. Jasmine broke into strained laughter. Here she was getting all stressed about a shirt that had been right in front of her nose all along. Now that she'd noticed it, she remembered getting warm—more by Christopher's gaze than the heat in the house—and shedding her flannel to work in her T-shirt.

The doorbell rang, and Jasmine jumped, putting a hand to her chest to still her racing heart. Why was it every time the doorbell rang in this place she jumped out of her skin? She'd be glad when this was over and she could sell the bungalow. The strain of Jenny's death was getting to her again.

She welcomed the charity people in, gesturing at the boxes to be taken. When one of the men picked up the apple box with her personal items in it, Jasmine reacted immediately.

"Wait," she exclaimed. "I'm sorry. That one's mine. I apologize. I meant to get it out to my car before you gentlemen got here."

The trucker, a boy in his late teens, grinned and handed the box to her. "Sure thing, ma'am. No problem."

She took the box and turned away from him before she scowled. She hated when people called her *ma'am*. It made her feel like her grandmother. And this young man was no exception.

Where did that come from, she wondered as she packed the box in the back of her four-by-four. She shook her head. It wasn't as if she were an old maid or anything. Lots of people established themselves in their careers before they married and settled down, didn't they?

Besides, she'd already had two bona fide offers of marriage, right? Okay, so both were from Christopher. But still... She tipped her chin in the air and marched back into the house, determined not to let it bother her.

"This is yours, miss?" the other trucker, a middle-aged man with jocular features asked, waving her flannel shirt. *Miss*. Now that was *much* better. She smiled widely. "Oh yes, that's mine."

She heard the crumple of newspaper as she took the shirt. The men would be there for a while loading the truck, she decided, and it would be best to stay out of their way.

She found an out-of-the-way corner where she could watch them without fearing they would trip over her, and sat down cross-legged on the floor. Gingerly, she felt for the pocket and pulled the newspaper clipping from it.

It was crumpled. She laid it against her thigh and smoothed out the wrinkles with the palm of her hand. The same proud man stared at her, and there was Jenny with her arms thrown around him and a silly grin lighting her face.

But there was love in her eyes as she looked at that man. Jasmine had no doubt of it now. Jenny had found true love, the way she had with Christopher.

Probably no one but a sister would notice. And it did make her wonder about Jenny's relationships before Christopher. The man in the picture obviously had money. It was odd that Jenny would settle for a penniless, small-town cowboy, even a guy as wonderful as Christopher.

Her skin tingled at the thought, and she shook her head. Back to the man in the picture. He was blond, buff, and, if the look on his face was anything to go on, conceited as all get-out.

She read the caption, searching for his name. "Barton Pembarton III," she read aloud, as snooty and regal as a butler announcing a guest.

She glanced back at the picture. "Barton Pembarton III enjoying a Valentine's Day cruise with his yacht *Celebration* on the Pueblo reservoir."

Of course, no mention of Jenny. She wasn't media material, even in a skimpy bathing suit. Jasmine wondered how Jenny had taken that slight, or if she'd even noticed. Perhaps she was used to playing second fiddle to the rich playboys she hung out with.

Jasmine, that's not fair! she chastised herself. She didn't know for a fact Jenny led that sort of lifestyle. She was the last one who should be judging another on circumstantial evidence, especially her sister.

She tucked her thoughts away with difficulty and returned her attention to the truckers. The men were finished with the boxes and bid her farewell on their way out.

There was a strange mixture of sadness and relief swirling through her chest at finally putting an end to all that was Jenny. It was almost as if she were being forced to say goodbye once again. She clutched the newspaper clipping to her heart.

The house was so empty and barren, devoid of life. Even the boxes had given it some sense of humanity. But now there was nothing. Nothing except herself and the photograph she held in her hand.

Chapter Thirteen

Jasmine glanced at it one last time, intending to tuck it into her wallet when she was through. She stared at Jenny for a long time, then ran her fingers over the caption.

Suddenly she noticed the date in the upper right corner of the clipping. *It was dated last year!*

Last year. Last Valentine's Day. But how could that be? She was with Christopher by then, carrying his child. Jasmine was a doctor—the math involved in pregnancy came naturally to her.

Sammy was born in early October, and he was two weeks overdue. That put his conception somewhere square in the middle of January. Which meant what?

She stared at the newspaper clipping in disbelief. Had Jenny been two-timing Christopher with this Barton What's-his-name? Christopher appeared to stiffen a little when he'd seen the photograph, but not nearly enough for her to believe he'd just discovered he'd been cuckolded.

He was a proud man. Whatever else he would do, he wouldn't accept his future wife out *playing* with another man. Besides, why would any woman want to cheat on Christopher? He was the most gallant, loving man a woman could want.

She swallowed hard, trying not to think of Jenny in Christopher's arms. She'd conquered her anger, but the stab of pain that accompanied any thought of those two together would never go away. Some wounds even time couldn't heal.

Jasmine turned her mind back to the puzzle at hand. Okay, so Jenny was pregnant with Christopher's baby and was hanging around with Bart. Where was Christopher?

She struggled to recall exactly when she'd learned about Christopher and Jenny's impending nuptials. She closed her eyes, trying to remember what she'd been doing when she heard the news.

Maternity. She'd been serving on the ward, learning firsthand how to bring new life into the world. And dreaming every time the miracle of birth happened of her own children, the ones she would have with Christopher.

Okay, technically, they weren't speaking to one another. And she was dating Richard, a radiology intern. But deep in her soul, there was only Christopher, and she knew she was kidding herself to be-

lieve otherwise. Richard was a nice, sweet guy, and
that was it. It was only pique and pride that kept her
from apologizing to Christopher and making things
right.

*She'd just finished a twelve-hour shift and was
getting ready to drop into bed when her phone rang.
Groggily, she answered, only to find Mrs. Rulitter
jabbering something about Christopher getting married and was Jasmine going to be able to make it
back to town for the wedding day, short notice as it
was, and all?*

*A dazed Jasmine had pulled the handset away
from her ear and stared at it, bemused. Of course
Christopher was getting married. To her. But it
wouldn't be until after she was finished with her
internship here in Denver. And anyway, it was
highly unlikely she'd miss her own wedding.*

*Mrs. Rulitter was spouting nonsense. She was on
the verge of telling meddlesome gossip so when she
heard something else on the line. The constant chat-
ter hadn't ceased. Apparently Mrs. Rulitter wasn't
even aware she didn't have an audience.*

*Somewhere in the prattle, she'd heard her sister's
name. Jasmine pulled the phone back to her ear and
cleared her throat loudly. When Mrs. Rulitter didn't
take the hint, she resorted to rudeness.*

*"I don't mean to interrupt you, Mrs. R., but I'm
afraid I missed what you said about Jenny. Is she
in some kind of trouble?"*

She couldn't imagine what her sweet sister could

have done to have become the object of town gossip.
Whatever it was, though, it was good and juicy
enough to warrant Mrs. Rulitter's long-distance
call.

"Has she asked you to be her maid of honor?"
Mrs. Rulitter answered a question with a question.

"Maid of honor!" she exclaimed. "Jenny is get-
ting married?"

"Of course. That's what I've been telling you.
Jenny and Christopher are going to tie the knot in
a month's time. Shotgun wedding, if the gossip—er,
news—I've gotten has the least inkling of truth.
Can't say I blame the girl. It's tough when you've
got a good-looking cowboy like Christopher."

Jasmine's head was spinning, and she sat down
hard on the bed.

"Shotgun wedding," Jasmine repeated dully, her
extremities going numb. Now she was not so much
afraid of passing out as simply turning into sludge
and melting into the sheets.

That meant a baby. Jenny was having a baby?
Christopher's baby.

She tried to breathe, but couldn't. "Are you sure
about this?" she squeaked through a dry throat
when she could speak again.

"Sure as shootin'," Mrs. Rulitter promptly re-
plied. "Jenny probably hasn't asked you to be maid
of honor yet because of—well, you know, your past
with Christopher. Bless me, I thought you and he
were gonna tie the knot. You sure were little lovers

*in high school. Oh well, I'm sure you both grew up
and grew out of each other. Happens all the time."*

Grow away from Christopher? Her every thought,
at least in her free time and often at work, was about
Christopher. But of course, that was how it must
look to an outsider.

It was almost laughable, if her stomach didn't
hurt so much. Jenny was bubbly and flighty. She'd
drive calm, cool Christopher mad in a day. And as
far as Jenny was concerned, surely she considered
Christopher as more of an older brother than a love
interest.

Lines were crossed somewhere. That was all there
was to it. She'd make a simple phone call to Gram's
apartment, and it would all be straightened out in
a heartbeat.

Or else she'd pinch herself **a**nd wake up. This was
more like a nightmare than reality. Christopher and
Jenny. What a laugh!

Or was it? Her mind flashed back to the night
before. She'd just come in from a date with Richard
when the phone rang. A glance at the call display
screen on her telephone warned her the call was
from Christopher.

Annoyed, she'd handed the phone to Richard and
requested he answer, knowing that would bother
Christopher more than any futile argument. Looking
back, she recognized how juvenile it was, and felt a
moment of regret.

It appeared his call had been much more serious

than she could have imagined. Had he called her to tell her he was getting married?

With shaky fingers, she punched the numbers on the keypad. She hoped Gram would answer. At least she would be straightforward. Gram always told the truth, no matter if it hurt.

The phone rang, then rang again. Finally, a light, tenor voice answered on the other end of the line. She might have thought she had the wrong number, but she recognized that voice instantly, and intimately.

Christopher.

She cleared her throat, suddenly flustered. Why was Christopher at Gram's house? Talking to him was even worse than trying to sort it out with Jenny.

She blew out a breath, hoping he couldn't hear how shaky it sounded. "Hi, Christopher. It's me."

"Jasmine!"

Under usual circumstances, she would have thought he was excited to hear from her. But what she heard in his voice was shock and alarm.

So it was true. Suddenly Jasmine knew, without his having to say the words. Their souls had been connected for so long she could even tell long distance what he was feeling.

"I understand I'm to wish you happiness," she said, trying but not succeeding in masking the bitterness lacing her tone.

She heard his deep intake of breath. "Jazz, I—"

She cut him off. *"Save your breath, pal. Let me talk to Jenny."*

"I tried to call you. I was going to drive up but—"

"Frankly, I don't really want to hear. Will you get Jenny for me, please?" she asked, annoyed that she couldn't keep her voice from shaking.

She'd heard Christopher curse as he put the phone down. He never cursed, and Jasmine felt a perverse pleasure in driving him to it. It was the least he deserved.

Jenny picked up the receiver, exuberant. *"Oh, Jasmine, I'm going to have a baby!"*

Nothing about Christopher, only the baby.

"So I heard," she said dryly. *"When?"*

"Well, Chris just took me to the doctor in Pueblo this morning. He says the baby is doing great, and I should expect her in early October. They did an ultrasound, and I got to see her little heart beating."

Jasmine had cringed at the use of Christopher's name. In elementary school, he'd given anyone who called him Chris a black eye. She'd always thought of him as her Christopher. But Jenny had broken all the rules.

"You know it's a girl already?"

"Well, no. Not really. I'm only ten weeks along. The ultrasound technician said she wouldn't be able to tell me the sex of the baby for sure until she was much bigger. And if it is a girl, they might not be

able to tell me at all. Little boys are easier to spot,"
she concluded, giggling.

*After that came the quick calculation. How long
had they been seeing each other behind her back?
It was Saint Patrick's Day, so Jenny had been seeing
him for at least two months, probably much longer,
since they were intimate.*

*Christopher simply wouldn't pressure a woman
on the first date. He'd never pressured her at all.
Maybe Jenny had pressured him. But in any case,
they'd been seeing each other awhile.*

*Yet he'd been with her, Jasmine, during the
Christmas holiday, which meant he'd been lying to
her. The time they'd spent together was a hoax.
He'd probably been with Jenny all along, right behind her back.*

*She'd felt as if gravity had tripled, pulling her
whole body down into the earth.*

*Jenny had filled the silence with her babbling.
"Can't you just see Chris bouncing all those curls
and pearls on his knee? Or teaching his little girl
to dance? He's going to be the greatest daddy in
the world."*

*She'd paused and waited for Jasmine to answer
her questions. As if Jasmine hadn't pictured Christopher as a father a million times.*

*"This is okay with you, isn't it? I mean about
Chris and me?"*

*Jasmine gasped for air, but her throat was closed.
"He said it would be. That you'd understand. I*

really hope you'll wish me happiness, Jasmine. It means a lot to me. And of course I want you to be my maid of honor at the wedding.''

A maid of honor. When she should have been the bride! she felt her head spin, and nausea was coming in waves. ''Yes, of course. Congratulations. Unfortunately, I'm calling long distance, so I won't be able to stay on the line. And I have a class in just a few minutes, anyway. Goodbye, Jenny.''

Jasmine had clanked down the phone in the receiver, grimacing at her lie. She had no class to go to. She was done for the day. She just couldn't stand to listen to the sound of Jenny's happy voice while she was in such agony. She lifted a prayer to God, asking Him to forgive her. She hadn't known what else to say.

She sank down beside the bed, seeking heavenly comfort. Only God could help her now. She'd been so exhausted when she first came into her room, but now she wasn't sure she'd ever sleep again.

After what had seemed like hours of praying and crying out to God, she'd dozed off, still on her knees.

Jasmine awoke with a start. The little bungalow was shrouded in darkness. Feeling displaced, she wrapped her arms around herself and took deep breaths.

She rolled to her knees, exclaiming as the cramped muscles in her neck, arms and thighs made themselves known in spiked bursts of pain.

Her voice echoed in the small room, making her feel even more alone. Something crunched under her left knee. Her newspaper clipping! She carefully set the clipping aside, then continued her slow, laborious crawl to the other side of the room. She reached the door and barely missed smacking her head against the solid oak before she reached the light panel. She flicked the switch, flooding the room with bright, cheery light.

Jasmine breathed a sigh of relief. She wasn't afraid of the dark, or of being alone, but the light was certainly welcoming to frighten away her dark thoughts. The day her own dreams died. A day she'd never forget.

March 17! Of course. That's what she'd been trying to remember. She dashed back across the room and snatched up the newspaper clipping.

She pieced it together in her mind, bit by bit, trying to create a timeline that made sense.

Sometime in early January, Jenny gets pregnant.

February 14, Jenny is seen on Barton the Snob's boat. At least he looked like a snob. She's clearly in love with him, or at least is making cow eyes at him.

March 17, she's engaged to Christopher.

She hadn't learned about the engagement all that long after it happened. Jenny had assured her they'd only made the decision to marry the night before. She went over the facts again. There was something she was missing. Jenny had cancer. Did she know of her illness at that point? Was she trying to live it up as much as possible before her death, even if she made Christopher suffer?

And Christopher—did he know about Jenny's illness? Is that why he allowed her to play around with another man? He wasn't the type of man to sit around blindly ignoring the obvious while he was being cuckolded.

Or…

Jasmine's thought was so astounding she felt as if her entire body had been pricked with thousands of pins and needles. Her blood pressure skyrocketed.

Or Sammy was not Christopher's son at all.

It made sense. Jenny and Bart. The thought was enough to make her cringe. Could Sammy's biological father be Barton Pembarton III?

She cringed, and her stomach swirled. That possibility was far worse than Christopher sleeping with Jenny, though that, too, must have been, or else why would he have married her?

The questions collided in her head like bumper cars. None of it made any sense, and yet it did. Too much so. And if Bart *was* Sammy's biological father, that created the possibility, however slight, of *his* claiming the boy, a thought that chilled Jasmine right to the core.

She shook her head, astonished. Things weren't anything like they appeared, and for every answer she concocted there arose five or six new questions.

Like why wasn't Bart in the picture now, if Sammy was his son?

Bart's son. That meant Christopher *couldn't* pursue custody of Sammy in court. He had no right if he couldn't prove his paternity. That he was married to Jenny would mean nothing, especially in light of his past behavior in running out on his wife and unborn baby. They'd surely ask him to take blood tests or whatever it was they did to check for DNA. And if the court didn't order it, she would, knowing what she now knew.

And if she could disprove Christopher, she would be free and clear to claim Sammy as her own. She'd work off the assumption that Bart didn't want anything to do with his son, or that he didn't know about him in the first place. She wasn't sure what was ethical in this situation, but she'd work that out later.

For now, she needed to find out the truth. And the one person who could tell her what really happened was Christopher. It was time to pay the man a visit and lay it all on the line.

The more she thought about it, the more she believed she was right, despite the nagging doubt that Christopher wouldn't take her to court in a custody battle if he wasn't absolutely certain he was the father of the child.

Well, there was only one way to find out. Confronting him would only save her the time and effort of having to go to court to make Sammy her son, if her hunch was correct. Sammy's adoption could proceed as scheduled, and her life could go on as well.

She refused to consider that life wouldn't truly go on without Christopher. She loved him, and she always would. It was more than likely she'd never marry. How could she, with Christopher always on her mind?

But she didn't have to be married to have a full life, did she? She had Sammy, and she had an exciting missionary vision she believed God had placed in her heart. Surely she could be happy with that. The question was, what to do now? She had to take *some* kind of action.

There was no way Christopher would continue this mad ploy to take her to court for custody if he discovered she knew the truth about him. About Sammy. No wonder he was so closemouthed about the whole thing.

She wondered again why he would take her to court when he wasn't the biological father. He had to know they'd demand a paternity test, and he'd be disproved in front of everyone.

Which meant, if everything she suspected was true, all his huffing and puffing about taking her to court was nothing more than a worthless threat.

The realization hit her like a bullet in the chest. Why that foul, no-good beast of a man! He wasn't really trying to take her to court to take Sammy away from her. That had *never* been his intention. He was bullying her into accepting his marriage proposal! It made perfect sense and explained nearly all his actions over the past month, save why he left Jenny after marrying her. *That* he still needed to explain.

And if he thought his little ploy to get her to tie the knot was going to work, he had another think coming. He was probably sitting around right this minute waiting for her to come begging for mercy.

Oh, she'd fulfill his wishes all right. She wasn't even going to wait until morning to pay that man a visit. But boy would he be surprised when she showed up at his door and cut the line to his threat like a snip with a pair of scissors.

She was out the door, her car key in her hand, when a thought occurred to her, one that put the brakes on her anger and sent her head spinning again.

If Christopher wasn't Sammy's father, why did he call him his son? And why did he want the baby boy as his own?

Chapter Fourteen

Christopher was tired of waiting.

He clamped his freshly shaved jaw closed as he pulled his left boot on, then his right. It was time for action. He'd considered and discarded a number of scenarios before settling on one. The right one. And the toughest.

He was going to tell Jasmine the truth. He stared at himself in the mirror, scowling at the man he'd become. A man of secrets. And what were secrets but lies left unspoken?

He should have told her the truth in its entirety the moment he'd crossed the town line into Westcliffe. No, that wasn't right. He should have driven up to Denver the second he and Jenny made their plans.

He *should* have talked to Jasmine before he made any plans at all.

He swiped a hand down his face and turned away from the mirror. A million *should-haves* wouldn't mend his broken world. He had to deal with the way things were now. And right now he had an irate, stubborn, wonderful woman on his hands that he couldn't decide whether to shake silly for being so headstrong or kiss thoroughly just for being herself.

He hoped for the opportunity to kiss her again. Over and over for the rest of their lives. But come what may, he couldn't keep up this ridiculous ruse and sit around waiting for her to come meekly and mildly offering to compromise.

He knew it wasn't Jasmine's style. He should have known it wasn't *his*. He'd spent the better part of the afternoon praying, asking forgiveness for his deception and for strength to reveal the truth to Jasmine when the time came.

He stuffed his cowboy hat on his head by the crown and adjusted the brim with his fingers. Now was that time. And it wasn't getting any easier by putting it off.

His mouth set in a grim, determined line, he opened his front door, then stepped back with a muffled exclamation of surprise.

"Jasmine!"

"Christopher." She was dressed in black jeans and a fringed western shirt. A small gold cross, set with a tiny diamond in the center, was the only jewelry she wore. Her long, shiny black hair was pulled back from her face with a clip, exposing her firm jaw and determined eyes.

If he didn't know better, he'd think he was looking at his reflection in a mirror. Jaw set, eyes sparking with stubborn pride and resolve, shoulders squared with purpose.

"Going somewhere?" she asked, gesturing to his hat.

"Er, yes. I mean, no. Actually, I was going to see you."

"You were?"

She looked every bit as flustered as he felt.

"Would you like to come in? The place isn't much to look at, but it's a roof over my head and walls to keep out the cold," he rambled, suddenly overaware of his humble surroundings.

"Not a problem," she said, shedding her coat and draping it across his armchair. She seated herself on the floor near the woodstove.

"Okay," he said, recovering slowly. He shut the door and tipped his hat off his head, returning it to the rack behind the door where he usually hung it.

He wondered where he should sit. If he sat in his armchair, he'd be sitting above her. Same with his desk chair. It might give him a slight mental advantage, but he wasn't sure that kind of advantage was what he wanted tonight. Then again, he was a gawky jumble of long arms and legs sitting on the floor.

But at least then he'd be face-to-face with Jasmine. He sat on the floor.

Actually, he stretched out right in front of her and propped his head on his hand, like he would have in the old days. With only a single lamp for lighting, it was dark, comfortable. Intimate.

"So…" Jasmine began, then stopped.

"So…" he repeated, feeling suddenly nervous.

"Did you want to go first?"

He swallowed hard. Did he? He probably should. She might have come to ask for compromise, which would be unnecessary once he'd spoken. But how did a man start such a conversation?

It was going to be a long night. Maybe he should offer her some coffee or something.

He took a deep breath and opened his mouth to do just that when she jumped in and beat him to the punch line.

"I could use some coffee." She gestured to a worn aluminum coffee percolator sitting cockeyed on the woodstove. "Is this the pot you use for coffee? You don't happen to have a microwave, do you? I don't much have experience with cooking on a woodstove. I'm a modern woman, if you know what I mean."

She was babbling, a sure sign that she was nervous. Christopher grinned inwardly and reached for the pot. "Now, don't you go fussin' over this here coffee," he said in his best imitation of John Wayne. "Why, this is the way the old cowboys used to make it. Threw the grounds right in to brew, they did."

She made a face, indicating she didn't believe him

for one moment. She still knew him that well, at least.

"It'll put hair on your chest," he drawled, laughing when her mouth dropped open.

"Oh. Now *there's* something I need," she said, laughing. "A furry chest."

Christopher felt himself blush to the roots of his chest hair. He coughed and made a bee-line for the door, unable even to come up with another line of conversation that would put the old one to rest.

Excusing himself, Christopher stepped outside to the pump and filled the pot with fresh spring water, then filled the aluminum cup with coffee from the barrel on the porch. Settling the lid on top, he took a deep breath.

Thankfully, she didn't follow him out, and he had a few moments to collect his thoughts and clear his head. He was going to be the first to reveal what was in his heart. It was imperative he be thinking about what to say, but Jasmine's presence made it excessively difficult for him to think of anything besides how much he loved her, how he wanted to take her into his arms and never let her go again.

It had startled him immensely when she'd shown up at his door at the very moment he was leaving to see her. But he had to admit in some ways it made what he had to do easier, in the privacy of his little cabin where they wouldn't be disturbed.

And she couldn't kick him out if she got mad at

him, he thought dryly. He chuckled, creating a puff of mist in the night air.

When he could stall no longer, he picked up the pot and returned to the cabin. She was seated where he'd left her, her arms wrapped around her knees as she stared vacantly at the warm glow of the wood-stove.

Seeing her there, her gorgeous black hair gleaming like silk in the dim light, he once again wondered how things could have gotten so far out of control.

He loved this woman with every beat of his heart. And he sensed that her feelings for him hadn't died, no matter how well she attempted to mask them with other emotions. He'd always been able to read her gaze, and he'd caught glimmers of what used to be in her eyes, especially recently.

But her eyes were shaded as they turned to look at him. Shaded, and angry. He wondered how her mood could have switched in the time he'd been outside, but he was afraid to ask.

Instead, he put the coffeepot to boil on the stove and seated himself on his desk chair. "Are you sure you wouldn't be more comfortable sitting on the armchair?" he inquired gently.

"No, thank you."

They sounded like strangers. It was enough to make Christopher want to pound something, but instead he leaned forward with his elbows braced on

his knees, clenching his fists behind his forearms so
Jasmine couldn't see.

She wanted him to go first, and go first he would.
"I needed to see you today, Jasmine, because—"

"Wait!" She stood abruptly and began to pace
the small room. "I don't want to hear it. All you've
ever told me about what happened between you and
Jenny are lies."

He shook his head in vehement denial, but she
held up her hands in protest when he tried to speak.

"Half-truths then. You're hiding something,
Christopher Jordan, and I've come here tonight to
find out what."

"Jasmine, if you'd let me explain," he interrupted, biting off his frustration before he lost his
temper. What was with her tonight, anyway? She
wanted answers to her questions, answers he was
finally ready to give, but she wouldn't let him get a
word in edgewise.

It was almost as if she were subconsciously trying
to avoid hearing what he had to say.

"Are you going to tell me the truth, or aren't
you?" she demanded, looking down at him with her
arms braced on her hips.

"I'm *trying* to tell you," he snapped back, standing to tower over her. "*If* you'd let me speak."

Her sparking green eyes widened slightly, then
narrowed upon him. She was not the least bit intim-
idated by his greater height.

"Good," she said firmly, reaching up and caressing his jaw with the palm of her hand, gently bringing his head down until his face was mere inches from hers. He closed his eyes, savoring the feel of her gentle fingers.

"Since you're in the mood to talk," she whispered, still stroking the line of his jaw, "Why don't you start with the fact that you're not Sammy's biological father."

Jasmine wouldn't have gotten such a strong reaction if she'd slapped him hard in the face. And in that moment, she knew that her theory was, indeed, fact. Christopher *wasn't* Sammy's biological father.

She'd come here with the intention of confronting him and being done with it. But she certainly hadn't meant for things to happen as they did. He'd stepped out to get water for the coffee, and she'd sat inside and stewed. It was a nervous reaction to coming face-to-face with him when he'd returned. He was standing over her, near enough to touch, his broad shoulders like a shelter. It had taken all her strength not to step into the haven of his arms. As it was, she couldn't help herself from touching his face, running her fingers across his clean-shaven jaw.

His cologne, a western scent, was strong, wreaking havoc on her senses. She'd almost succumbed to the love she still felt beating strong in her heart.

And then she remembered the impassable wall between them, the wall created by Jenny. And Sammy.

She'd just blurted out what she knew with no warning, no warming up to the subject.

Christopher had exhaled as if someone had sucker punched him and whirled away from her, raking his hands through the tips of his short brown hair. He stood facing away from her, and she could see his hands trembling.

"I see you're not denying that you really aren't Sammy's biological father."

"How long have you known?" he asked, his strained voice a good octave lower than his usual smooth tenor.

"I only began suspecting it this afternoon. I didn't know for sure until this moment." In an instinctive move borne of love, she stepped forward and reached out for him, stopping just short of touching him.

"I guess you're really laughing now, aren't you? I played my trump card and lost everything."

He sounded so genuinely miserable that Jasmine flinched. What he said was true, but she knew she had put some of that agony in his voice. Oh, *why* hadn't she gone home and spent the night praying before blustering up here like a misguided whirlwind?

She muttered a quiet prayer for God's help to untangle the entire mess once and for all. Then she reached up and gently placed her hands on his shoulders. "I'm sorry, Christopher," she whispered, her voice cracking. "I shouldn't have blurted it out that way. I've hurt you."

He stepped away from her touch and turned to

face her. Instead of the tortured expression she expected to see on his face, she found him scowling so darkly she took an instinctive step backward.

"Don't apologize, Jazz. I've had it coming for a long time. I'm not surprised that you loathe me."

"I don't—" she began, but he cut her off.

"It's time for you to hear the whole story. It isn't pretty. But it's time you knew the truth."

Jasmine sighed. "Well, at least we agree on one thing."

He led her to the easy chair and bade her sit. Reluctantly, she did, and he knelt before her. It felt too much like a knight paying homage to his queen for Jasmine's tastes. She would have preferred to be on an equal level. She tried to move onto the floor, but he wouldn't let her.

He took her hand and turned it over, palm up, staring at it so fiercely it was almost as if he were trying to find the answer to their dilemma in the lines of her palm.

"I'm asking for forgiveness, Jasmine, though I don't expect you'll be able to give it right away. I want you to—" his voice cracked and he paused, swallowing hard "—to be able to put this episode behind you. To go on with your life and...find happiness."

This sounded like a eulogy. Jasmine's heart sank. She'd been so angry. She still was. But even so, she wasn't sure she was ready to say goodbye to Christopher forever.

God was calling her to missionary work in Ecuador. She'd have to say goodbye to Christopher one way or another. But it just didn't feel right.

"Go on," she said at last, when he didn't continue.

"I also want you to know I never meant to hurt you."

She lifted an eyebrow. That was pushing things a little bit. He had, after all, dumped her for her sister and then—but no, Sammy wasn't his baby.

"It might not seem that way now."

She nodded, barely restraining a bitter laugh. Lately she'd discovered nothing was as it appeared.

"I told you how Jenny called me one night, asking me to come to dinner with her and Gram. Gram wasn't there, and Jenny was a wreck."

Jasmine pictured the scene in her mind. "I remember. You said she was throwing things."

"Yes. She was hysterical. Completely beside herself. But Jasmine," he said, his voice low and earnest, "that night—it was the night I tried to call you and that guy answered."

"What?" she shrieked, then clapped a hand over her mouth. "I thought—"

"That the night in question had been much earlier. Otherwise, how could I have been Sammy's father?"

"But you're not..."

"Exactly. Anyway, to continue the story, I calmed her down and we watched a movie. After the movie, Jenny was herself again. She told me the real reason she invited me over. She needed help. She—'' Again he cut off his sentence.

"She was pregnant with Barton Pembarton the Third's baby,'' Jasmine concluded, the scene coming clear in her mind. "She'd tried to call me, but I wasn't home. I remember the message on my machine, now. It said to call her right away, but I was pulling an all-nighter.''

She had closed her eyes as she pieced the facts together, but snapped them open when Christopher's hands closed firmly on her arms.

"How did you know?'' he asked in amazement.

"How did I know what?'' She was having trouble following him, steeped as she was in chronologizing the facts.

"Know Pembarton's name?''

"The newspaper clipping we found in the drawer. Remember?''

"Yeah. That's the first time I'd ever seen what he looked like.'' He clenched his hands. "Man I'd have loved to give him a piece of my mind.''

Jasmine chuckled. "You'll have to stand in line. I expect there's a number of people in that category.''

"When Jenny told him about the baby he refused to acknowledge it.''

"What?'' Jasmine stood. "Why, that—''

"That's not the worst of it.'' Still on his knees, Christopher reached for her hands and drew her down beside him on the floor. "He told her he was engaged to marry a Denver socialite. His parents' choice for his bride."

"Poor Jenny," Jasmine whispered.

"Well, you can understand why she was so upset." He looked away. "And she'd learned she had cancer and didn't have long to live. I didn't even know what to say."

"I can imagine."

"I was her sister's boyfriend. I felt so awkward even discussing such private issues. But she was hurt, and needed to talk."

"Is that what she wanted you to do?"

"Yes. She already loved her baby, and despite everything, loved the baby's father. It was her family she was worried about—the stigma of her having a child out of wedlock."

"She should have known we'd all stand by her and support her."

"Yes, but Westcliffe is a small town. Things like illegitimate children are remembered forever. It isn't like Denver where single moms are the norm and a person can just fade into the background."

"That still doesn't explain how you and she ended up together," she reminded him, bracing herself for the answer she'd been waiting so long to hear but in truth was afraid to know. "Or why."

"I thought it was the right thing to do, that God had placed me where He did for that reason," he said with a bitter laugh. "I thought it's what *you* would have wanted me to do."

"Marry my sister and not tell me about it?" she snapped, the old hurt rising to the surface. He'd known about Jenny's cancer. "Where did you get a cockeyed idea like that one?"

He blew out a breath and looked away. "I meant to tell you everything." Suddenly he stood and pulled on his jeans to straighten them. "Coffee's ready. You still want some?"

"I guess." She looked away from him. Coffee didn't even sound good anymore.

He returned with two steaming mugs and handed her one before sitting back down. He propped one arm on the seat of the easy chair and sighed. "Jenny was more concerned for you and Gram than she was about her own reputation. And of course, she worried about the baby."

Jasmine drew in a loud breath. Of course Jenny would think of Sammy first. Hadn't she been that way the whole time she was pregnant?

Christopher continued. "She didn't know what to do. She was just talking it all out, really, trying to come up with a feasible solution that wouldn't hurt anyone."

Her breath froze in her chest. Did they really think their actions wouldn't hurt anyone? Did they not consider the ache ripping through her heart when they planned all this?

But of course, Jenny had sacrificed so much more.

She'd given her life for her baby. Who knew but that chemotherapy would have prolonged her life, perhaps even saved it?

Jenny hadn't so much as mentioned her cancer to Jasmine. Did she fear Jasmine might try to change her mind? But how, *how* could she have believed it would be okay to marry Christopher?

"I was the one who convinced her," he said, answering her unspoken question. "She wanted nothing to do with it, not knowing what you'd say, how you'd feel. But I knew you'd understand, so I talked her into it."

"You knew I'd understand," she repeated dumbly, wondering why everyone else in the world presumed to know what she would think and feel when she couldn't even figure that out herself.

"She was young, alone and scared. And pregnant. If we announced our engagement, everyone would just assume the baby was mine. He'd have a name, and he'd have my protection."

He paused and made a fist. "Bart Pembarton was a weak, irresponsible boy, still tied to his mother's apron strings. I wouldn't let him near someone I care for, much less a baby. Jenny knew it as well."

"Then why was she with him?" Jasmine blurted angrily. "Where was her head, Christopher, for her to go and get pregnant by someone like Bart?"

He pinned her with a glare. "That's exactly what the town would have said. Don't you see that?" She was shocked into silence.

"He's dead now, so the point is moot."

He didn't say how Bart had died, and Jasmine didn't think to ask. The news only added to the depth of her wounds. Poor Jenny. She'd been so fortunate that a man like Christopher would come into her life when he did, would offer her the solace of his name and take on the burden of her illegitimate child.

"That explains who, what, where and why," she said, ticking the list off on her fingers. "But there's one thing you haven't answered."

He lifted an eyebrow.

"How were you planning to handle *me? Oh, Jasmine, by the way, I decided to marry your sister instead of you?* Only you never got a chance, did you? Because dear old Mrs. Rulitter thought she should be the one to break the news to me."

"Oh, come on, Jazz," he snapped, his face flushing. "Give me a break, here. I'm sorry you had to hear it that way. But that's not how I meant it to be. You know I tried to reach you."

Jasmine stood and crossed her arms to stave off the chill settling in her heart. She was trying to understand, she really was. But the sense of betrayal that she'd been struggling to tamp down just wouldn't stay put. It bubbled up in jealous swirls all around her insides.

"Tell me then, Christopher, how it was supposed to be."

"Yeah, well, think about this, Jasmine. What if

you had been there that night? What if you had picked up the phone and heard Jenny wailing on the other end? What if she had told *you* her story. What would you have suggested she do?''

The air seemed to get thicker in the room. Her mind raced for a pithy answer, or even a serious one, but nothing came.

''Yeah, that's what I thought,'' he drawled. ''It was the only thing I could think of. And it would have worked. If things hadn't gotten out of hand so fast.''

''Meaning if I hadn't found out the way I did.''

''Well, yeah, sure, that's what I mean. I tried to tell you. But obviously, I didn't succeed,'' he finished miserably.

''Just for curiosity's sake, what were you planning to say? Were you just going to break things off with me and leave me dangling?''

''Of course not!'' he nearly shouted, then looked away. ''I was going to explain everything. You were supposed to see how heroic I was being, and how perfectly everything would turn out. I mean—'' he cleared his throat ''—as perfect as things could be, under the circumstances.''

''In spite of the fact Jenny was dying.''

''You're still not seeing the whole picture, are you?'' he demanded, thrusting his fingers through his hair.

''Evidently not,'' she said wryly. ''I haven't quite figured out how I was supposed to play into all this.

Or whether I was just supposed to fade out of the picture completely,'' she added on a pique.

"You were supposed to marry me, you mule-headed woman!" he stormed. He stalked across the room and leaned one arm against the wall.

She laughed out loud, but it was a dry, bitter sound. "Oh, I see. You were going to be a bigamist. That surprises me. Somehow I always pictured you as a one-woman kind of guy."

"I am," he declared, the passion of his statement making his neck redden. He was by her side so quickly she didn't even see him move before he swept her into his arms and kissed her firmly and thoroughly.

She was breathless by the time he raised his head. His eyes were glowing with conquest. Her heartbeat roared in her ears, and she thought if he let her go, she might well fall to the floor.

Never in all their years together had Christopher kissed her with such strength and passion. To her surprise, she wanted more. If he leaned down and kissed her again, she wouldn't so much as mew a protest.

But he didn't kiss her. He gently pushed her away and into the easy chair, where he knelt before her.

"I'm a one-woman man," he said, his voice husky. "And I always have been. Jasmine, that woman is, was and always will be you."

"But you married Jenny, anyway." She could have slapped herself once the words were out of her mouth, but she couldn't help it. Her wounds were recently reopened and raw to the touch.

He tipped her chin so their eyes met. "Yes. I did. And I'd do it again. Jenny was dying. She wanted you to raise the baby. She knew I was going to marry you, so it was the perfect solution. I would marry Jenny and proclaim myself the legal father of the baby. When she died, you, Sammy and I would be the family Jenny wanted us to be. She really loved you, you know. You were supposed to be in on the plan."

Tears rolled down her cheeks at the thought of her sister sacrificing everything for her baby. And all Jasmine had been able to think about was the way she'd been jilted. Her sister hadn't told her about the cancer, and now, perhaps, she knew why. Jasmine had backed away from her relationship with Jenny, letting her sense of betrayal get the best of her when she should have been trying to forgive.

She should at least have been trying to find out the truth. She hadn't even done that. How many actions had she based on misconceptions? How much hurt could she have spared everyone? She knew Jenny suffered from the breach in their relationship at least as much as she had.

Maybe more.

And how much more she would have made of the short time with her sister. If only she had known.

"You okay, Jazz?" Christopher asked uncertainly, reaching for her hand.

She snatched it back and cradled it against her. She was so ashamed of her words and actions, she could barely think. "Why didn't you just tell me the truth?"

He groaned. "If you remember, we weren't exactly on speaking terms when we first saw each other again. I lived in constant fear of flying projectiles."

She couldn't even find it in her heart to chuckle. Her sorrow was nearly overwhelming, and she knew if she didn't escape Christopher's cabin soon, she'd break down completely and wouldn't be able to go anywhere.

"And then it became too difficult. Insult piled on insult until no one could break their way through." He paused and wet his lips with his tongue.

"I'm as much at fault as you."

"I was going to tell you everything the day I came back to Westcliffe. But then when some of the facts came together, I stood to lose Sammy. I knew you'd be a great mother for him, but I just couldn't rest until I was part of the picture. I wanted Sammy to have my name. And my protection, what little I could offer."

"But he's not your son. You could have just walked away." *Like you did before.* But she didn't need to say the words.

"That boy is my son, Jasmine, in every way that matters. I love him, and I want to take care of him. I didn't want him—or you and Gram—to face any more scandal than you'd already dealt with. And I guess I didn't really want to be the one to have to tell you about Jenny. Or that Bart's parents rejected Sammy as their grandchild. It seemed easier to remain quiet.''

Revealing Jenny's shame would only add another scandal to the family record. Dear Christopher had done all he could to shield the Enderlins from harm. It just appeared that they—*she*—got into trouble faster than he could play the rescuer.

''I've got to go,'' she said suddenly, snatching up her coat and dashing out the door without looking behind her.

Christopher called to her, but she refused to listen, to stop her headlong flight into the darkness of the night. It was where she belonged, in the dark.

She knew the way back to her four-by-four, and her feet put themselves one in front of the other without conscious thought.

He'd given everything, and she'd done nothing. She hadn't proved her love with faith and trust. Instead she'd made every one of his gallant actions twice as hard for him to make.

He must hate her. And if he didn't, it was only because he was the best, kindest, most honorable man in the whole wide world.

And she didn't deserve him.

There was a new wound in her heart, one that made the others small by comparison. She wanted to cry but her eyes were dry, for what use was crying when the wound in question was self-inflicted?

She was every kind of fool. And she'd discovered the truth too late.

Chapter Fifteen

So much for confessing the truth, Christopher thought, lifting himself gingerly from his easy chair. It was very early in the morning, judging from the thin stream of light beaming through the window. He'd spent the night half-sleeping, half-praying on the chair, and every muscle in his body was screaming for release.

And he was no closer to resolution than he'd been when Jasmine had left the night before. He didn't know what he expected God to do.

He knew better than that. God wasn't going to solve his problems for him, or undo the mess he'd made. A man had to live with the consequences of his actions, even when it meant watching the woman he loved walk out on him.

He deserved it, of course, but that didn't make it any easier to swallow. To have fought so long and hard for their happy ending, and then to have it dashed from his hand by his own foolishness was its own penalty.

She wasn't coming back. He'd seen the disillusionment and disappointment in her eyes, heard the anger sounding from her voice. She no longer trusted him.

And not all the words in the world could unscramble the disaster that his life had become.

Heading out the door the night before, his heart had been light. He'd found hope that she might hear what he had to say and forgive him. That they might have that happily-ever-after ending they used to dream about. Sammy would only add to their bright future.

His chest clenched, thinking about Jasmine and the baby. Despite the circumstances, God had given him such a love for baby Sammy he could barely contain it. It was like a fountain overflowing. And now he'd lost Sammy, too.

He found himself at the stable, where he looked around uncertainly. It occurred to him that here was a good getaway, to ride off into the Sangres until he figured out what to do next.

He had plans, at least. He'd felt God's call into ministry. He finally knew what he wanted to do with his life. But he'd hoped with all his heart his future would also include Jasmine and Sammy.

A dark bay nudged Christopher with his muzzle and he jumped back, laughing shakily. "Guess you just want some hay, now, don't you, fellow?'' he asked, not knowing if he spoke aloud to reassure the beast or himself.

"Hey, Chris. Whatcha doin' in the barn?" Old Ben, one of the ranch hands sidled up to him and slapped him on the back. "Goin' riding?"

"Thinking about it," he admitted, sliding a glance toward Ben.

"Kinda green with horses, ain't ya?"

He chuckled. "You could say that. I've been on a horse all of twice in my life."

"I still don't see how you could have been raised on a ranch in Westcliffe and don't know how to ride."

He sighed quietly. This wasn't his week. He was going to have to divulge another secret just to get a horse. "Twice being when I fell off backward," he clarified. "I was six."

"Shoot, boy, you should've climbed back on. Who was teaching you? They should've known that."

"Unfortunately," he commented dryly, "I was teaching myself. And as far as I was concerned, taking one topple was enough to prove I wasn't cut out for the rodeo."

"But you want to ride now." It was a statement, made with an undertone of humor.

"I expect so. If you'll help me saddle a horse, that is."

"Well, I'd hate to keep a cowboy from his cows,

if ya know what I mean. But I gotta tell you, I don't have a broken nag in the bunch.''

"You don't have a single horse I can handle?'' Maybe this was a bad idea and he should take his truck up to Horn Lake or something. At least his truck wouldn't throw him off. But for some reason, maybe it was guilt, he wanted to ride a horse.

"Commander might be a safe bet,'' he said, stroking the white stubble on his jaw. "Recently gelded. Ought to be a safe ride.''

"Which one's Commander?''

"This dapple gray over here.'' He reached into his pocket and produced a carrot, which he fed to the nickering gelding.

Christopher tugged his hat lower over his brow and set his jaw. Commander. Sounded intimidating to a man who didn't like horses. He reached out a hand to stroke the horse's muzzle, but quickly withdrew it when he bucked his head and whinnied.

Old Ben laughed. Christopher scowled.

"Are you *sure* you don't have another one for me to ride?'' he asked, ready to give the plan up completely. "I only want to go up by Horn Lake for a while.''

Old Ben scratched his head, then his eyes lit up. "As a matter of fact, I think I *do* have something you can handle.''

"What's his name?''

"He's a she. And her name's Fury.''

Fury. And he'd thought Commander was bad.

* * *

A good night's sleep could make a world of difference to a woman, Jasmine reflected as she rose and glanced at the clock. Nine o'clock. She never expected to sleep as well as she did. It was amazing how clean a freshly scrubbed soul could feel. She'd come straight home from Christopher's cabin and slipped into the apartment so as not to wake Gram or Sammy.

She'd dropped into bed, exhausted from thinking and sobbing. So depleted, in fact, that she wasn't sure she had enough left in her to pray. Which is why it surprised her at how easy confession came from a quiet mind.

She didn't have to speak aloud and list every sin, or kneel in the proper posture of prayer and make her pleas to heaven from there. She merely had to lie still and *be*. God did the rest, sweeping in and taking the burden away from her, replacing it with the peace that passes understanding.

Be still and know that I am God.

The Scripture had soothed her wracked nerves, unhinged the stress from her shoulders. She'd made a thousand mistakes, but God was greater. Thank God, He was greater.

This morning, all that was left was to go back to Christopher, this time for good. She'd unjustly condemned herself, she realized now. Yes, she'd made more than her share of mistakes, but then again, so had Christopher. Surely they could forgive each other and finally be at peace.

She laughed out loud. He was every bit as stubborn as she was, the big lug. They'd butt heads more than once during their marriage, but she couldn't think of a rosier future or a brighter dream. She'd have the two men she always wanted, Christopher and Sammy, to love and spoil for the rest of her life.

"Where are you going looking so chipper, young lady?" Gram asked suspiciously as Jasmine entered the living room where Gram was rocking Sammy, who sucked noisily from his bottle.

"Hey there, little guy," she said, kissing Sammy on the forehead and Gram on her weathered cheek. "And hello to you, too, lovely Gram."

"Now I know something's up," she complained good-naturedly.

"I'm going to see your daddy! Yes I am!" she said in baby talk, as Sammy wrapped a pudgy hand around her finger. "Daddy's going to take good care of his little boy."

"Now, this *does* sound interesting," Gram said with a crackly laugh. "Do tell."

Jasmine couldn't help but smile. "I love him, Gram."

"Oh, now *there's* news."

"And I think he loves me, too," she concluded with a sigh.

Gram rolled her eyes. "And it took you *how* long to figure that out?"

"He's not the bad guy in all this."

"I never said he was," Gram reminded her.

"No, I guess you didn't. But you never offered me an easy way out."

"The easy way out isn't always the best way out. The road is narrow, and that sort of thing. Besides, I didn't know anything for certain. I just suspected that young man of yours wasn't the type to change his character so radically. He's always been a good fellow, that one."

"Oh, he's that," Jasmine agreed with a laugh. "That, and *so* much more."

"You've ironed out all the issues?" she asked gently. "Come clean with each other?"

"Well, pretty much. I guess." She experienced a sudden flash of apprehension running through her, but it abated as quickly as it came.

"Good. Then you can tell me why he left Jenny before Sammy was born, especially since you knew she was dying. That's the one thing I've never been able to figure out."

She blanched. "I...er...that's one of the things we haven't discussed yet."

"Jasmine," Gram exclaimed in exasperation. "Don't you think that's one of the biggies you want to have cleared up before you make any long-term plans with the man?"

"Well, yes, sure," she agreed, stammering slightly. "But Gram, the point is, I trust him. I don't know why he did what he did, but I trust that he had a good, honorable reason for doing it."

Gram raised a bushy white eyebrow, and Jasmine held up her hands in her own defense.

"Even—maybe especially—about his leaving Jenny."

"I cannot even fathom."

"Well, neither can I. But I'm not going to speculate, either."

"There you go, girl," Gram said, her voice filled with encouragement. "You're off to see him, then?"

"Yes, after I check on Marcus at the clinic. I need to have a long chat with him, anyway."

"Just don't get distracted," Gram teased.

"Oh, Gram! You know I won't. There's nothing to keep me away from Christopher now."

She made a beeline for her four-by-four, hoping to corner Marcus as fast as possible and be off to see Christopher. She still hadn't mentioned to Marcus that she wanted him to be her permanent replacement, but then it occurred to her that she hadn't yet mentioned Ecuador to Christopher, either.

Well, of course she hadn't. They weren't exactly on speaking terms. She couldn't just blurt out that God was sending her to a foreign country to work as a missionary. And it could be that Ecuador would have to wait.

She felt it so strongly, so certainly in her heart, this need to serve as a doctor in that little hospital in Quito. But if God allowed her to be with Christopher, she would choose that first. If God really meant her for Ecuador, the rest would fall into place in His time.

For once she would trust God and see what happened. It could only be good. She was certain of that.

She was more nervous about speaking to Marcus than she was to go see Christopher. Somehow she felt she'd deceived Marcus, and perhaps she had at that.

She found him in a back office, cheerfully working on a pile of paperwork higher than his head. He was singing a hymn under his breath and tapping his pencil in time to the beat.

"You can take the man out of the music, but never the music out of the man," she said with a laugh.

He looked up quickly, a startled look quickly replaced with a welcoming grin. "You said it, girl. Don't be thinking you'll be takin' the music out of *this* man any time soon."

"It's good to see you so happy," she said gently, her heart welling up with joy.

"I've never been so content, Jasmine," he agreed, placing a hand on her shoulder. "I'm glad you brought me out here. New York wasn't the place for me. I just didn't know it."

She smiled up at him and gave him an impromptu hug, which he returned.

"I told you God changes your dreams. Now all I

want is a small country clinic like this one and a roof over my head. Beautiful mountains on one side and a gorgeous valley on the other.''

"I've been meaning to talk to you about that dream," she inserted, taking the opening.

"Oh, so the time has come already. You feel rested enough to get back to work?"

"No, no," she exclaimed, shaking her head fervently. "I didn't mean that at all. I was wondering if you'd like to stay on here as *this* clinic's doctor!"

His face brightened immediately, but then his brows fell in confusion. "You know I'd take this job in an instant," he said, his voice low even for him. "But if *I'm* the doctor, where does that leave you?"

"Happily unhindered and pursuing the Lord's work," she replied promptly.

"Huh?" he asked, justifiably confused. "But I thought *this* was the Lord's work for you."

"Maybe it was. But not anymore." Her excitement bubbled over, and she smiled widely. "I'm getting married, Marcus!"

"To Christopher, I assume," he commented, sounding mildly cynical.

"Well, he hasn't asked yet—again—but I'm hoping he will today. And I plan to accept. There's more," she said, and she proceeded to fill him in on her plans to go to Ecuador to be a missionary.

Marcus laughed aloud. "Girl, you better be goin'

to tell your honey that information right away. That isn't the kind of news you surprise him with on your wedding night.''

"I know. I'm on my way to see him now. I wanted to see you first."

"Tell him I wish you both the best."

"I will, Marcus. Thanks." She blew him a kiss and dashed out of the clinic, eager to find Christopher and throw herself into his arms.

Nerves finally hit her as she walked up to Christopher's cabin. She hadn't actually planned what she'd say when she got here, and now she could think of a million reasons why she shouldn't be there at all.

She knocked on the door and waited, tapping her toes in time with the hymn running through her head. The same hymn Marcus had been singing, she realized with a smile.

When he didn't answer, she searched his empty cabin, then headed to the mess hall. Frustrated and feeling her anxiety rising, she decided to find a moment's peace and shade inside the stable. She inhaled deeply despite the crisp air. She loved the smell of horses.

Quite a contrast, really. Next to the hustle and bustle of a hospital emergency room, there was nothing she liked quite so much as the respite of a stable, with its pungent combination of fresh hay and fresh manure, and the horses stamping and whickering lightly in the background.

She walked up to a friendly gray and rubbed her hand along his neck, making soft, horsey sounds with her tongue. She'd been riding since she was three. Though they didn't own any horses now, she occasionally borrowed a mount from here at the Walters to take a picnic into the mountains.

"That's Commander," said a voice from behind her.

She jumped and put a hand to her pounding heart. "You startled me, Ben," she said, turning back to the horse. "Well, there, Commander, aren't you a pretty boy?"

"That he is," Old Ben said fondly. "The poor fellow was recently gelded, so he's still got some stallion to wean out of him. But he'll be an excellent mount after a month or two."

"Yes," she said, speaking to the horse. "I'll bet you'll be a beauty, won't you, my boy? I'll have to take you on a ride sometime so you can show off what you can do, won't I, big boy?"

Old Ben laughed behind her shoulder.

"What's so funny? I've been riding since I was three," she said, offended.

"It's not that, Jasmine. I know you can handle this mount. But this morning—" He snickered and wiped the corner of his eye with the sleeve of his flannel shirt. "This morning, Christopher Jordan wanted to ride Commander." He promptly burst into another round of laughter.

Jasmine knew it was polite to laugh along, but she couldn't. She didn't know what jolted her more—the fact that Old Ben had seen Christopher this morning, or that the crazy love of her life wanted to ride a horse!

"You didn't let him, of course," she prompted.

He chuckled again. "Not on your life. The guy was heading into the hills. Said he wanted to go up by Horn Lake. On a *horse*. Oh, man."

Jasmine smiled along with him as her mind processed the information. Christopher was clearly trying to find somewhere quiet to think things through. Up to that point, he was being rational. But why on earth did he want to ride a horse, when he could just as well have driven himself up to Horn Lake?

"Thanks for not giving him a mount," she said, smiling at Old Ben.

His pale blue eyes widened and he scratched his day's growth of beard. "Oh, I gave him a mount."

"What?" Jasmine screeched, clasping her hands together.

"Sure." He smiled. "I put him on Fury."

"I don't believe this." She turned and stomped out of the barn, heading straight to the mess hall. Christopher was somewhere in the Sangre de Cristo mountain range on a horse called Fury. And he was alone.

Ben might think it a joke, but to Jasmine, Christopher on a horse was deadly serious. He knew nothing about trail riding, and there were a million hazards to best even a good rider.

After getting Cookie to pack a lunch for two, Jasmine rushed out the door and made her way steadfastly back to the stable. Ben stood where she'd left him, looking bemused.

"Don't just stand there," she barked. "Help me saddle up Commander."

He raised his eyebrows at the order, but did as she requested. Jasmine ran back to her car for a few emergency items she always kept with her and stuffed them in the saddlebag. Ben had already tied her lunch to the other side.

"You going to be warm enough?" he asked, concern in his eyes.

Jasmine picked up the reins and led Commander to the front gate. The horse had a nice, easy pace, and Jasmine didn't anticipate any trouble. "I expect so, Ben. Don't worry about me."

"Okay, I won't," he responded, walking out beside the horse. "But, Jasmine—"

She cut him off with a "Hee-yah." She set off at a canter, leaving the stable, and Old Ben, in the dust.

The last thing she heard as she turned around the corner of the drive, was Old Ben muttering, "—about Fury…"

Chapter Sixteen

Christopher lay flat on his back with his hands clasped behind his head, staring at the clear blue Colorado sky. A cushion of snow and pine needles made his bed a comfortable one, and it wasn't too terribly cold with the sunshine streaking through the trees.

God's country. He didn't get up here enough to ponder God's creation and wonder at His magnificence. It sort of put things in perspective for him.

His life was in God's hands, and he wouldn't have it any other way. He'd apologized to Jasmine, and tried to set things right. That was all he was able to do. He regretted the fact that he'd let his temper get the best of him, but he supposed he'd apologize for that too, when the time came.

He was trying to imagine a life without Jasmine and Sammy, but it just wasn't fathomable. They *were* his life. But he'd done everything he could to make them a family, and everything he'd done had failed. He could only hope for a miracle, now.

In the meantime, he supposed he should go on pursuing the call God had given him for the ministry. He'd put his application in to the local seminary, right here in the Sangres, only about a mile from where he currently lay. The president of the seminary had already assured him of a spot in the next class, which would start at the beginning of summer.

At least he would remain close to Jasmine and Sammy this way. He couldn't even consider not being able to see his son, and his dear, sweet Jasmine on a regular basis. He thanked God again for the blessing of Sammy, who would bind him to Jasmine forever, in a way, even if it wasn't the way he would have chosen.

He heard the sound of hoofbeats approaching only seconds before Jasmine launched herself from the saddle and landed in an ungraceful heap of arms and legs right on his chest, knocking the breath from his lungs.

If the shock of her landing didn't stun him, the fact that she was feathering kisses across his face and neck certainly did. And there were streams of tears rolling down her cheeks. He stared up at her stupidly, unable to move.

"Oh, my darling Christopher. Oh, my dear, crazy love. I came as soon as I heard. I brought supplies in the saddlebag. Oh, just tell me where you're hurt, my love, and I'll make it better.'' She was half laughing and half sobbing as she continued to rain kisses down upon him.

It occurred to him that he didn't really *want* to move, or to be taken from the heaven in which he'd suddenly found himself. He had no idea what Jasmine was about, but as her silky hair fell down around him, he thought he might have found the most pleasant way to smother to death that the world had ever known.

She stood up as quickly as she'd descended on him. For a moment she just glared down at him, then turned and stomped to her horse, yanking a paper grocery sack off one of the saddle strings.

She stomped back and threw it at him, again pelting him in the chest. He grinned despite his best efforts, and swung to his feet, casually leaning his back against a convenient pine tree.

''I thought you were injured,'' she said, enunciating each word unnecessarily, ''because Old Ben told me he let you ride out on Fury. And—''

He tried to interrupt her, but she held up her hands and continued on.

''*And* there you were, lying on the ground like some corpse or something and I thought... Oh! Who cares what I thought? The point is, you're fine.''

''You sound as if you'd rather I wasn't,'' he remarked dryly.

''At this point, don't push it,'' she said, and then broke into laughter.

He laughed with her, relieved. Apparently she was here with some purpose other than to cause him bodily harm. They met each other's gaze and laughed even harder. He reached out and hugged her to him, wanting her back in his arms. She didn't resist.

"Uh, Jazz?" he asked when they'd both somewhat recovered. "About Fury..."

"You must be a better rider than I thought. Or else a quick learner."

He shook his head and tried not to grin. "Not exactly."

She lifted an eyebrow, and he shrugged and pointed to the glen, where Fury was tethered.

Jasmine had been honestly terrified when she tracked him up here, but she turned her gaze to where he pointed and felt her mouth drop open in surprise. "That's *Fury?*"

An ancient gray donkey with one droopy ear looked back at her, his expression one of mild annoyance. He had a clump of grass in his jaw and was chewing slowly. He couldn't move beyond turtle speed, she was certain of that just by looking at him.

At least now she knew why Old Ben had been laughing. "He's a little short for a man with your long legs, don't you think?"

Christopher turned a deep shade of red, and reached to retrieve his cowboy hat from the ground.

"Fury is a she, thank you very much, and it just so happens that we got along fine."

"In other words, no one saw you trying to ride the beast," she teased.

He tugged on his cowboy hat and grinned from underneath it. "That, too. But really, she's perfect for me. One speed, slow. And since my legs can almost touch the ground when I ride her, I don't have that *liable to take a digger* sensation I get from riding a horse."

"Oh, Christopher." Before she could consider her actions, she slid forward, framed his face in her hands, and kissed him soundly on the lips. She loved him, every crazy inch of him, and she wanted him to know that.

"I didn't think you'd be back," he admitted, settling her into his arms. "I was trying to figure out what to do next."

"And what did you decide?" she murmured, locking her arms around his waist and snuggling under his chin. "There's food in that bag, by the way."

"Then we should eat. I missed breakfast this morning."

"Yes, I know." Kneeling, she ripped the sack open to bare the contents—fried chicken, cheese, biscuits and a couple of apples.

Christopher shined up an apple on his flannel shirt and took a big bite. "You make it your business to know whether or not I eat breakfast?"

"I make it my business to know a lot of things," she teased. "Like how you planned to get along without me."

"I couldn't do that, and you know it. You and Sammy are all the world to me. But—" he paused and stared down at his apple.

Jasmine felt her chest tighten, as if she were once again going to lose control. But control wasn't hers to begin with, she reminded herself. It belonged to God.

"What I was thinking about up here," he said, crouching down to face her, "is that I'd like to go to seminary. In fact, I've applied to the one here in Westcliffe. I believe God is calling me to the ministry."

She took in a deep breath, then laid a hand on his arm. "Oh, Christopher, that's wonderful." She stroked his forearm up, then down again, loving the texture of flannel under her fingertips. "Are you going to pastor a church?"

"I'll do whatever I have to in order to stay near you and Sammy, but—" He removed his hat and swept a hand through his hair before planting the hat firmly back in place, brow low over his eyes. "But recently I've had other ideas with what I might do for the Lord."

"Such as?" She sensed his hesitance, and wondered if she ought to tell him she'd follow him to the ends of the earth if necessary. That was, after all, what true love was about.

Still, though Christopher was being affectionate enough, he'd spoken of being *near* her and Sammy instead of *with* them. She kept her thoughts to herself and her mouth firmly closed.

"I want to go to Ecuador, Jazz. There's a hospital there where you could do some work if you wanted. After I left Jenny, I got an EMT certificate in Pueblo."

"So *that's* where you learned to deliver a baby," she said, the lightbulb in her head going off.

She was still reeling about his wanting to go to Ecuador. It cleared up any lingering doubts she had about whether or not the two of them should be together, but she wasn't quite prepared to express her thoughts in words. For now, she simply wanted to experience the sheer joy of a match made in heaven.

After a moment, she sighed aloud. "Will you be angry if I ask you a question?"

He sat down beside her and laced their fingers together, squeezing gently. "I love you, Jazz. I want to marry you. If there's anything else we need to clear up between us, let's get it over with now. Let's start fresh from today, okay?"

"Okay." Her heart thumped loudly in her chest as she wondered how to phrase the delicate question. "I want you to know up front that it doesn't matter what you say. I love you and I'll marry you, and the answer to this question isn't going to make a bit of difference."

His Adam's apple bobbed as he swallowed. "It means a lot to me that you trust me."

"I do. But there's no sense in leaving a nagging question behind. Why did you leave Jenny, Christopher? Everything else makes sense, seen from your viewpoint. You acted in a gallant and honorable manner. But then how could you leave?"

She held her breath, wondering if she'd been too harsh.

He smiled gently, and sadness lurked in his eyes. "Another thing I didn't want you to know about Jenny." He blew out a breath. "She knew when I married her that my heart did and always would belong to you. She knew I planned to tell you, though the thought humiliated her. But you had to know, for the baby would one day be your own."

"Yes, but you didn't tell me."

"No, I didn't," he replied gravely. "And because I didn't, Jenny got it into her head that I might come to love her, and that the three of us might be a real family."

"I can see how that would happen." It hurt to think about it, but Christopher was a magnetically attractive man. What woman could sleep with him and not fall prey to his natural charm and stunning good looks?

"She was young," Christopher explained. "And idealistic. I tried to ignore the tension building between us, but she wouldn't let us be. One day she demanded that I—well, uh..."

Understanding dawned on her, and she swiped a hand down her face as if clearing the cobwebs. "What are you trying to say, Christopher? That you didn't consummate the marriage?"

"That's exactly what I'm trying to say. Jasmine, you didn't think that I'd—"

"I'd think that if you gave me no reason to believe otherwise."

"I love you, and I've always loved you. We made a pledge long ago to save ourselves for each other, and I've never broken that promise. Not even when I made my pledge to Jenny."

Tears pricked at the corners of her eyes. After all this time, all she'd been through, they would still have the joy of a previously unexplored wedding night together.

"The long and short of it is, Jenny threw me out. She was in love with me and couldn't bear the thought that I was in love with you."

"But why did you leave? Everyone blamed you." *She* had blamed him, when all the time he'd been suffering for her.

"One takes the bow, one takes the blame, Jasmine. That's just the way things are. Jenny threatened to expose herself if I didn't leave town. She told me not to contact her at all, and not to ever try to see the baby."

"Do you think that was jealousy talking?"

"Oh, I'm sure it was. And immaturity. I'm not holding a grudge."

"Another man would," she said, feeling as if she were missing some fact, something important that was lurking just outside her reach.

"I'm not another man."

"That's the understatement of the year." She hugged him close and closed her eyes. Jenny's face sprang to mind, just after she'd had Sammy. Her last words—she was trying to say something about Christopher.

"I love you, Jazz kitten."

"I love you, Christopher cat," she replied, using the pet names they called each other in high school. "And honey?"

"Mmm?" he asked, his face buried in her hair.

"I think Jenny wanted us to get back together. At the end...she kept saying your name."

"There you go, then. Happily ever after."

She smiled, knowing he couldn't see. It was time to share some of the joy in her heart with him. "Not completely, my dear."

"No?" He leaned down on one elbow and looked up at her, his normally gray eyes a smoky blue, shining with love for her. "What have we missed?"

"Oh, something about Ecuador."

He smiled up at her. "God will work it out in His own time, if it's meant to be," he said, reaching a finger up to stroke the line of her jaw.

She leaned into his caress. "He already has. I've had my application to Quito in for months now. I'll just tell them to put me on hold for a couple years so you can finish seminary and I'll continue to work part-time at the clinic with Marcus.''

"Yeah?'' She put a hand to his chest and could feel his heartbeat pumping wildly. "Well, praise God!''

"Yes, let's,'' she said, smiling.

"Marcus is going to stay and work at the clinic?'' he asked belatedly.

"Marcus found he has a liking for country living. We've already made arrangements for him to stay on here.''

"*Now* can we have our happily ever after?'' he whined like a petulant little boy.

"*Now*, my love. And let's not rush it. We have the rest of our lives together.''

Epilogue

Considering the fact that the Enderlins were still in questionable social status, nearly everyone in town showed up for Jasmine's wedding three weeks later—the soonest Christopher and Jasmine had been able to convince Gram she could arrange a proper wedding.

The church was so full they were bringing folding chairs in, and it occurred to Jasmine, as she stood in the back of the room to watch the proceedings, that perhaps they should have used the grange hall.

But of course she wanted a church wedding, with her pastor decked out in his finest vestments up in front, and she gliding up the aisle in her white gown like a fairy-tale princess.

She felt like a princess, on this happiest of days. The only sadness to mar the event was that her parents and sister were not here to see her wed to Christopher. She wondered if they could see their loved ones from heaven, if they knew that today was her wedding day.

People quieted as the organist began the wedding march. She had no bridesmaids, as a sign of respect to her sister. She tightened her grip on Marcus's arm and bowed her head, saying a little prayer of remembrance.

"Hey, girl, you aren't nervous, are you?" he whispered, sounding surprised. "This here's your big finale."

"No it's not," she whispered back, scowling. "It's only my grand entrance."

"Touché," he said, and bowed. He was handsome in a white tux with tails, especially when he smiled in that big, toothy way of his. "We're on."

Jasmine gathered her dress and her thoughts, but in the end, all she could think about was putting one foot in front of the other. She didn't even look up until she reached the front row, and then she was so stunned she couldn't think at all.

Christopher stood waiting, his eyes alight with love. In his arms, in a matching silver tux with ruffles and gray cowboy hat, was his son. He'd insisted Sammy be part of the ceremony, and Jasmine was glad he was. Now she was walking up the aisle to her two handsome men, and her future couldn't look any brighter than this moment.

Marcus patted her hand as they reached the front, and the minister held his hands up for silence. He intoned the requisite opening and asked who would be giving the bride away.

"I am," Marcus boomed in his resonant bass. "In place of her mother and father, and in memory of her sister."

He placed Jasmine's hand in Christopher's, and she was relieved to feel his own hand shaking beneath hers. Or maybe it was her hand shaking them both.

"Thanks, buddy," Christopher whispered as Marcus moved away.

He turned back and winked at them both. "You take care of my girl, Mister."

Usually Christopher would have bristled, but today he merely grinned. "You can count on it."

The minister directed them to face one another and hold hands in order to exchange vows and rings. Jasmine had seen a dozen real weddings and who knew how many more on television, but she had no idea how completely her life would flash down to this one moment. She was certain she wouldn't be able to say a word.

"Are you ready?" Christopher whispered, squeezing her hands.

"I've been ready for years," she whispered back.

It seemed only moments later that the ceremony was complete and they were turning around to be introduced for the first time as Mr. and Mrs. Christopher Jordan. And their son Samuel. The many times she'd dreamed it as a teenager didn't hold a candle to the real thing.

Tears ran unbidden down her cheeks, but she didn't even bother to wipe them off. They were here, the three of them, a family at last.

"Happy, my love?" he whispered in her ear.

"Oh, yes."

"Then promise me you'll never look behind, but only to what's ahead." He gestured down the aisle and out the door, to where a limousine waited to take them to the airport.

It was an easy promise to make. And one she intended to keep.

* * * * *

Dear Reader,

The apostle James tells us the tongue is a fire, and likely to burn out of control if we aren't careful what we say. Sometimes, however, it's what we don't say that gets us into trouble.

That's what happened with Christopher and Jasmine. Assumption built on assumption and was never confirmed. Pretty soon it became impossible to tell what was truth and what was a lie.

I hope you enjoyed journeying with Christopher and Jasmine. As is always the case when an author puts her fingers to the typewriter to create characters, I ended up learning more than they did. It's my very great privilege to be able to live with my characters and share in their conflicts—and, of course, their resolution.

I love hearing from my readers. Please feel free to write me at P.O. Box 9806, Denver, CO 80209.

Blessings,

Deb Kastner